PROPERTY OF

FEDERICO IVANIER

SWORD OF FIRE

Translated by Claire Storey

A PUFFIN BOOK

PUFFIN BOOKS

UK | USA | Canada | Ireland | Australia
India | New Zealand | South Africa

Puffin Books is part of the Penguin Random House group of companies
whose addresses can be found at global.penguinrandomhouse.com

www.penguin.co.uk
www.puffin.co.uk
www.ladybird.co.uk

Penguin Random House UK

First published in Uruguay by Alfaguara as *Martina Valiente* 2004
First published in Great Britain by Puffin Books as *Sword of Fire* 2025

001

Set in 10.5/15.5pt Optima LT Pro
Typeset by Falcon Oast Graphic Art Ltd
Printed and bound in Great Britain by Clays Ltd, Elcograf S.p.A.

The authorized representative in the EEA is Penguin Random House Ireland,
Morrison Chambers, 32 Nassau Street, Dublin D02 YH68

A CIP catalogue record for this book is available from the British Library

ISBN: 978–0–241–68879–3

All correspondence to:
Puffin Books
Penguin Random House Children's
One Embassy Gardens, 8 Viaduct Gardens, London SW11 7BW

Penguin Random House is committed to a sustainable future for our business, our readers and our planet. This book is made from Forest Stewardship Council® certified paper.

MIX
Paper | Supporting responsible forestry
FSC® C018179

For Joaco and Seba

Federico Ivanier is an acclaimed Uruguayan writer for young people. He has written over twenty books that have been published across Latin America. His works have been awarded the National Prize for Literature from the Uruguayan Ministry for Education and Culture, a Cuatrogatos Foundation Award, and the Premio Bartolomé Hidalgo, one of the country's most important literary awards. As well as writing books, Federico works as a high school English language teacher.

Claire Storey translates from German, Spanish and Catalan into English, specializing in literature for young people. She has translated books from Uruguay, Argentina, Mexico, Spain, Germany and Austria. Claire regularly volunteers in schools talking about careers with languages and was named Outreach Champion 2021 by the UK Institute of Translation and Interpreting.

Contents

Novrogod. Wizardry. The Butterfly of Light. Martina had never heard of any of these before, let alone the Sword of Fire, a fiery blade that was said to burn even beneath water, turning everything it touched to ash. But even if she had been told about them, she would never have believed such things could be real.

And yet – know it or not, like it or not, believe it or not – all that was about to change . . .

Slave Traders Ca
Lipax River
Rope Bridge
The Crazy Skull
Village of the
Crescent Moon
Kelytong

Black Rock
Desert of Nothing
Caves
N
NOVROGOD
River of Dark Waters
S

One
The Wanderer in the Darkness

The Wanderer in the Darkness descended through the air, held up by invisible strings. Although his black cloak melted into the shadows, Martina could still see him. His long-fingered hands, a pale and sickly white, shone like a ghost. Even though she couldn't see his eyes, Martina knew he was looking at her. Her heart was pounding.

The Wanderer in the Darkness. She had given him that name the first time she had seen him. He carried a wooden staff as tall as he was, topped with a sphere, and he used it to dominate the world. Martina didn't know where she'd got that idea from, but she was certain it was true. Just as she was convinced that he was looking for her, that he had been from the very beginning, each and every night, from dream to dream. He was waiting for her.

Sooner or later she would have to face him. She thought hard, imagining she could fly, and – whoosh – her feet simply lifted off the ground until they were face-to-face.

'Martina . . .!'

A flash of lighting cut through the darkness. Hands rested on her shoulders.

'Martina . . .!'

She opened her eyes.

Her mum was watching her, dressed in a yellow shirt, her hair swept into a messy ponytail.

'Martina, wake up!'

Martina glanced around the room, her bedroom. Her *new* bedroom. It felt different to her old one, but this was home now. Or at least it had been for the last couple of days. Martina squinted, dazzled by the light.

'All right, Mum. I'm awake.'

'You were rolling around and sleeptalking. What *were* you dreaming about?'

'I don't know. I can't remember.'

She'd never told her mum about the Wanderer in the Darkness. Not once. She'd always had these nightmares, ever since she could first remember. She didn't know where they came from, and she'd never mentioned them to anyone. Talking about them, even in the daylight, sent a shiver down her spine.

Her mother sighed, then said, 'Do you want a glass of water or anything?'

'No, nothing. I'm fine.'

'Are you sure? You're all clammy.'

'Yeah, I'm fine.'

Her mum gave her a calming smile. Over the last three months, what with the divorce and the house move, her mum's face had become lined with small wrinkles. She tried hard to pretend these furrows didn't exist, but Martina could still see them, perfectly so, even though they were never talked about. Just like the nightmares.

'It'll all be all right, you know?' her mum said with a smile. 'The new house, the new neighbourhood, all these changes. It'll all be fine. You'll see.'

'Yes, Mum.'

'Your new school will be great, and you'll get to know lots of new people. And you'll get used to seeing your dad a little less, and –' she looked up, as if looking at the house – 'Basically, you'll just get used to everything.'

'Yes, Mum.'

'You're much stronger than you think.'

Martina smiled, more to make her mother happy than anything else. So far she hadn't made any new friends, and she hadn't got used to seeing any less of her father. In her humble opinion, things were not going well.

'Right, well, I'll leave the light on. If you need anything, give me a shout.'

'Mm-hmm.'

'Relax and try to sleep.'

'OK.'

Her mother left the room and Martina was alone again. She wasn't sleepy any more and she didn't feel like reading. She climbed out of bed, stood next to the window and opened it. Outside, there was a pleasant breeze, the dark sky was full of stars and the moon looked like a white cat curled up asleep in the sky. Martina took a deep breath, inhaling the scent of the night, and leaned against the windowsill.

It had only been two days since they had first set foot in Grandma Famke's flat in Montevideo, but it felt like a lot longer. They had opened the door on that hot, sticky day at the end of January and Martina had peered inside. Before anything else, a smell of confinement had filled her nose. The house beyond was dark, and the dust floating in the air had been illuminated by the sunlight pouring in through the open door. She had simply stood there, her shadow cutting into the rectangle of light falling on to the pale, worn parquet flooring, a long and slightly scrawny outline, her curly hair falling to her shoulders.

Having just turned twelve, Martina Adler wasn't much to look at, or so she thought. Narrow shoulders, a slim neck, red hair (unbrushable), her face covered with freckles (as was the rest of her) and a slender body. Her legs were slim, too, and when viewed as shadows they looked like two slender poles. Sometimes Martina worried about her weight; she was the skinniest of all her classmates. Well, her old classmates, at least: Gabriela, Magdalena, Mariana, Stefanía.

Martina and her mum had moved to the district of Buceo on the other side of Montevideo, an hour away from where her friends all still lived in Prado. Before, it had only taken her five minutes on her bike to go and see them. Now it would take her ages. And all because her parents were getting divorced. Her dad had gone off to live with an accountant called Silvia who had a fourteen-year-old son called Matías and a thirteen-year-old daughter called Nicole. Her mum had decided she didn't want to stay in their old house on Buschental Road any more, so there they were, in Grandma Famke's old house in Buceo.

Mysterious Grandma Famke . . . She had died before Martina was born and had come to Uruguay from Europe, fleeing the Second World War. Martina knew why she had fled, but not exactly where Grandma Famke had come from – somewhere in Europe, that's all she knew. At the end of the war all that had remained of her village was rubble. Everything had been destroyed.

Martina's first impressions of her new home had been depressing. The house had been full of dust and the sofas were covered in cloths that might once have been white. The living room was large, but it had only added to her bad impression of the place. The paint had been flaking off the walls and mould had spread like a faint bruise in the corners of the room.

But the thing that had caught Martina's attention the most that first day was the mirror. It was huge, with an ornately carved frame. *That must be really valuable*, she'd thought. Its polished surface had been covered in dust, like everything else, and it had been difficult to see anything in it. Martina's own reflection appeared like a ghost wearing red shorts, a black T-shirt with a smiling sun and moon overlapping above a 'No Te Va Gustar' sign – one of her favourite Uruguayan rock bands – and simple sandals. For a second, it had startled her that she didn't completely recognize her face. Perhaps the lights in the house – or the shadows – were playing tricks on her. Or was it the mirror? Most likely, it was how fast she was changing: the child she'd once been was beginning to disappear.

'Is this really where we're going to live?' she had asked.

'Yes, Martina. Right here,' her mother had replied.

'But we can't live *here*.'

Her mother, Ariana, was a translator of French and English for the Libyan Embassy. She had placed her own freckly arm round her daughter's shoulders and sighed, looking about.

'That's what this place wants us to think, isn't it?'

Cobwebs had hung from the ceilings and the whole place reeked of melancholy; it was difficult to think it *wanted* anything. But even so, the thought had made her mum smile.

'But we won't let it fool us!' she'd added.

Then she had flung open the windows. Light and fresh air had filled the rooms, welcome guests that had been absent for many years.

That night Martina had handed responsibility over to some greater force, trusting that the roof wouldn't come crashing down on them as they slept. It had seemed the place might just fall apart like a giant house of cards, but it had stayed standing. The wooden staircase leading to the upstairs had not fallen through and Martina had chosen one of the three bedrooms on the upper floor to be hers. The window offered a splendid view of the sky.

Over the next few days, carpenters, builders, plumbers and a painter had come in, and huge bags of rubble had gone out. The Wanderer in the Darkness seemed to have followed her there, invading her dreams, true, but he couldn't stop them from doing up the house. That felt good. And he certainly couldn't stop Martina from exploring the house. Or exploring its contents. That also felt unexpectedly pleasant, even homely. During the afternoon after the nightmare, on the third day in the house, Martina found several old toys that were beyond salvation, as well as some other bits and pieces that she was unable to make neither head nor tail of. They were in the wardrobe in Martina's room and she hadn't liked any of it, so she had planned to throw it all out.

'We're not getting rid of all these toys!' her mother had exclaimed. 'Some of them could still be useful.'

'Useful for what? They're broken,' Martina had replied.

She had known she had a point – and her mum had known that too.

'Some of them . . . I don't know, remind me of things . . . But you are right.'

'Besides, they're really ugly,' Martina had continued, holding up a doll wearing a musty outfit. 'This one's definitely going.'

At the time of the conversation, Martina's bedroom had been half painted and a ladder had leaned against a wall covered with white splodges of wall filler.

'Mum, what's this?' Martina had asked.

She had been holding up a golden metal cube. It was covered in dirt, but beneath the grime it had gleamed.

'Where did you find it?' her mum had asked, looking at it. It was fairly heavy and cold to the touch.

'In there,' Martina had said, pointing to the wardrobe.

'To be honest, I don't remember that at all.'

'What's it for?'

'I don't know. People used to display photos in cubes.'

'What do you mean by *in cubes*?'

'Not like this metal one – they were made of plastic. You inserted a photo in a slot on each face, so there were six photos in all, one on each side.'

'People used cubes instead of photo albums?'

'Many still do, as far as I know.'

'I've never seen one. Ever.'

Her mum had smiled, looking thoughtfully at the cube. Her image was reflected on the surface, a somewhat distorted version of herself.

'They're like frames, but they hold several photos at the same time. People leave them out on sideboards or shelves.'

'Oh,' Martina had murmured, and picked up the cube again. She'd wiped the dirt off one of the sides and looked at herself. The face of a freckly redhead had looked back at her. The cube had seemed like a nice knick-knack, though. 'Can I keep it?'

'Of course,' her mum had said as she ran her fingers through Martina's hair. 'I don't see why not. Finally, something you don't want to throw away! Do you like it?'

'Yeah . . . I dunno, it's strange. I have no idea what it's for, but I like it as a trinket. I could even stick some pictures to it.'

'You're going to damage it if you cover it in stickers –'

'Muuum!'

Martina had looked at her mum and seen her laugh, her head thrown back, the way she used to. Martina had inwardly thanked the golden cube and became even more certain that it should live next to her bed.

She'd also found a bedside table that she wanted. It was an old wooden one with curved edges and grapes carved into the door. Since then, Martina had sanded it down to remove the damp and given it a couple of coats of varnish, and now it looked like new. It even smelled good. They'd also found an old metal lamp in the shape of a candle. It didn't work, but they'd sent it off to be fixed, bought a lampshade for it and *ta-daa*!

Martina had chosen the colours for her bedroom and the curtains, too. Once everything had come together the room became fresh and bright, and she had begun to fill the walls with posters. She had one of the album *De Bichos y Flores* by rock band La Vela Puerca, and another of the film *Rock of Ages*. Her dad had got her that one the last time he went to Los Angeles, and even though Martina had never actually seen the film, she still liked the poster.

After five days of hard work Martina's room had felt much more orderly, which secretly made her very happy. At night, she had no dreams of the Wanderer in the

Darkness – at least, she hadn't for the last few days. She didn't even think much about it. She slept facing the new bedside table on which sat the lamp and the mysterious golden cube that had put her mum in such a good mood.

Two
Riddles and misunderstandings

'*What?*' asked Nicole. Her cutting tone came naturally; there was no need to pretend. At thirteen, Nicole was the queen of contempt. 'Why does *she* get to have *that room*?'

She, in that particular conversation, was Martina, who was due to visit later on. And *that room* was the attic in their house. Nicole, her brother, their mum and Martina's dad were eating dinner while seated round the wooden table in the kitchen.

'Because nobody's using it,' answered Matías, as he stood up and went over to the fridge.

Matías was Nicole's older brother, but he lacked the contempt of his sister. He spoke in a much calmer, flatter tone of voice. He carried a jug of water back to the table and sat down. He walked easily; his skin was lightly tanned from the sun and his quiet green eyes moved slowly. He was relatively tall for his age, with solid, well-set shoulders.

'I mean, it's not even a room,' Matías added. 'It's an attic.'

'It *is* a room. I use it to store all my old stuff.'

'What stuff?'

'Clothes, magazines, *stuff*. Where am I going to put it all now?'

'How about in *your* bedroom?'

'Oh really? Would you like to tell me where?'

'Oh no! You're gonna have to throw some stuff out. How awful.'

Nicole glared at her brother over the table.

'Mu-um . . .' she whined.

'Kids, kids,' Silvia intervened. 'We're just trying to find a solution. That's all.'

'I *need* that room!' insisted Nicole.

'Great, perfect,' said Matías. 'That's all sorted then. You keep the attic and Martina can sleep with you in your bedroom.'

'My bedroom?'

Matías sighed, worn out by the conversation. However, the decision was quickly made. For now, anyway, Martina would have the attic when she stayed with them on the weekends.

Silvia spoke to her daughter. 'We all have to make some sacrifices. Martina is our guest, and –'

'Well, really, if this is her dad's house then she's not *actually* a guest, is she?' interrupted Matías. 'Doesn't that make it her house too?'

Matías didn't wait for an answer and instead moved straight on to a different topic of conversation.

By the time Martina arrived, one week after her last dream with the Wanderer, Nicole had plastered a huge movie-star smile on to her face.

'Hello, Martina,' she said. 'How are you?'

Martina's dad smiled happily. Martina frowned. Nicole's welcome seemed odd, but she let it go.

'Fine, thanks,' she replied.

'Come on, let me show you –' Nicole took a deep breath before she was able to utter the next words – 'your new . . . bedroom.'

'OK.'

Nicole took Martina upstairs. Once they got there Nicole showed her around the room. There were several cardboard boxes piled up in one corner and a mattress on the floor that was made up for her bed, with some folded towels on top. A shaft of light slanted in through the small, single window at one side.

'This is it,' said Nicole. 'D'you like it?'

'Erm . . . yeah.'

'I've been trying to sort it out so it would be ready for you when you got here.'

Nicole wafted her head from side to side, shaking her silky blonde hair, which floated down and came to rest around her shoulders, just like in a shampoo advert.

'Thanks. You've got gorgeous hair,' said Martina.

'Well, yeah. What about yours? Why have you got it all tied back?'

'Well, erm . . . I can barely even get a brush through mine!' Martina giggled.

'Let's see. Take it down.'

Martina smiled and after a moment's hesitation took the hairband out and tried to pat her hair down. Nicole pursed her lips while she studied Martina's red hair.

'Yeah, too many curls. Probably best you tie it back up again. Well, anyway, settle in, and when you're ready, come back downstairs.'

At dinner time they gathered in the kitchen and, to help break the ice, Martina's dad, Miguel, decided to set them a riddle.

'So, who can guess this one?' he asked. 'It goes like this: Who is the person who is your parents' son or daughter, but isn't your brother or sister?'

'I know, I know,' shouted Nicole.

'Let's hear it then.'

'I'm just thinking. I swear I've got it though.'

Matías crossed his arms and looked at his sister.

'Hold on, just say it again,' Nicole insisted.

'Who is the person who is your parents' son or daughter, but isn't your brother or sister?' Miguel repeated.

'So?' asked Matías.

Nicole glared at her brother. 'I'm nearly there, all right. Don't rush me!'

'You either know it or you don't,' said Matías.

'Yeah, well, clearly I do,' snapped Nicole.

'Excellent. Spit it out then,' Matías said, looking at her, barely pursing his lips.

Nicole huffed. 'They don't exist,' she said finally.

'Of course they do,' said Martina's dad. 'If they didn't, it wouldn't be a riddle.'

Martina, who had always been fascinated by riddles in general, and somehow felt she had a knack for them, thought she had this one.

'That person . . . is me,' she said.

'No,' said Nicole. 'Don't be ridiculous. How's it going to be *you*?'

'Very good, Martina,' her dad said. 'Perfect! Well done!'

'That's not fair,' said Nicole. 'She'd heard that one before.'

'Actually, I only heard this riddle today,' said Martina.

'I mean, that's exactly what I was going to say,' said Nicole. 'It's just too obvious. When someone's your parent's daughter and it's not your sister, it's gotta be your stepsister.'

'Huh?' said Miguel.

'Exactly. It's just so obvious.'

Martina smiled and Matías started laughing.

'Erm, not quite, Nicole,' said Martina's dad. 'The answer isn't *stepsister*, or *stepbrother*. As Martina said, the answer is *yourself*.'

'What d'you mean, *yourself*? So, me?' asked Nicole.

Matías's guffaws echoed off the kitchen walls.

'Don't laugh!' said Nicole.

'When you apply the riddle to yourself, then yes. Who is the daughter of your parents but isn't your sister? It's you. There isn't anyone else.'

Matías was now laughing out loud.

'Shut up!' yelled Nicole.

Matías ignored her.

'Mu-um!'

'Kids, kids . . .' soothed Silvia.

'You're so thick sometimes. Jeez,' said Matías as he wiped away a tear, still laughing.

An hour later, resting back against the pillow, Martina was writing in her diary.

Dear Diary,

Sometimes I don't know which is worse: being alone in my new home or being here. I remember my old room, the one that looked out into the garden. Now I don't have a garden or a bedroom.

Martina had bought the diary about two years ago when she was ten, shortly after starting her fifth-year classes. In the beginning she'd just written in it every so often, but gradually she'd started adding to it more and more. And during her parents' divorce she had taken to writing in it every day.

Sometimes she read back over what she'd written. For example, on the twenty-ninth of June the previous year, just before the school holidays had started in July, she'd realized she fancied Paco in 6B. He had blue eyes, was almost a head shorter than her and hated maths.

Back in the present, the door to her attic room opened. It was Nicole.

'Hi Nicole,' Martina said as she closed her diary and smiled.

Nicole closed the door, stormed over to Martina and grabbed the back of her hair, forcing her to look upward.

'Make that the last time you *ever* try to make *me* look stupid, d'you hear?' she snarled.

'Let go, you're hurting me.'

'Did you hear what I said?'

'You're hurting me!'

And it wasn't just her scalp. She felt a distinctive tingling sensation at the base of her neck, between the shoulder blades – right where she had a red birthmark hidden by her long, red locks. It was as if something was heating up, right then and there, on her skin.

Meanwhile Nicole simply wouldn't let go.

'Did you hear or didn't you?' Nicole asked.

Martina raised her hand, buried her fingers in Nicole's hair and pulled with all her might. Nicole screamed and released Martina, who also let go, leaving Nicole's hair tangled and sticking out.

'Sorry, Nicole, it's just –'

But Nicole carried on yelling as if she was being murdered alive. Martina didn't know what to do. As Nicole carried on screaming her head off, they heard footsteps thundering towards the attic.

Silvia burst in, followed by Martina's dad. 'What happened?' Silvia demanded.

'I came to have a chat with her and she started pulling my hair,' cried Nicole, clinging to her mother.

Martina looked at the scene and thought, *You must be kidding me.*

'Martina . . .?' her dad asked.

The redhead looked at him, pleading with him silently, *What? Don't tell me you believe her?*

'Why did you do that?' pressed Silvia.

'I didn't do anything,' Martina said, but even as she spoke, she knew Nicole had the upper hand. Martina would never be able to put on a show quite like that, even if she tried.

'Martina, what's going on?'

Her dad peered at her through his glasses. His hair was black and swept into a side parting. He usually wore an easy smile, but right then he wasn't smiling at all. They were in the kitchen, alone together.

'Nothing,' responded Martina.

'And all that business upstairs in your bedroom?'

Martina shrugged. 'It's not even a bedroom.'

Miguel sighed. He was a psychiatrist, and a fairly successful one at that. However, it seemed to Martina that sometimes he treated her like one of his patients.

'Martina, I know, it's a time of change for all of us, and change can be difficult . . .'

'*I* didn't change anything,' Martina said, folding her arms.

'I didn't say you'd changed anything. I'm just saying we're all going through a lot of changes together: a new home, Silvia, Matías, Nicole . . . even finishing elementary school and starting high school is a change. You'll meet new friends –'

'I never wanted any new friends! I like the ones I had!' Martina exclaimed.

'Well, even so, this is just how it is. And, however you may be feeling, you can't just walk in here and start pulling other people's hair.'

Martina clenched her teeth. She wanted to leave, but she didn't know where to go. Somewhere far away.

Her father leaned back on the chair and sighed while Martina sat there, her arms folded across her chest. Just then the door opened, and Martina sat up a little straighter.

Matías came in. He walked calmly over to the fridge, looking straight forward, as if nothing else was going on, his long hair tucked behind his ears. He took out the bottle of orange juice and glanced at Martina, as if seeing her for the first time. Martina exhaled slowly.

'Anybody need anything?' asked Matías.

'We're fine, thank you,' said Miguel.

'Martina?' insisted Matías.

'I'm OK.'

'Good,' he said, and smiled.

Somehow, that simple gesture made Martina realize she was fine enough.

Matías looked away again, picked up a glass and disappeared with both it and the bottle of juice.

'Martina . . .?' Miguel said.

She turned to look at her father. 'I get it, all right? I won't hurt anyone else. Can I go to my room now?'

As Martina made her way there, she found Matías waiting for her, drinking his juice.

'Next time, rough her up a bit more. But you defended yourself well for a first go.'

And silently, he slid away.

Things calmed down over the next few weeks, though they weren't great. At her dad's, her bedroom wasn't even a proper bedroom – it was more of a room with a bed – and Nicole truly hated her. Both of her parents were obsessed with work, especially her mum. She often had translations to do at home – far more than she used to do. And that was on top of her work at the Embassy.

This meant that Martina had to make her own breakfast – her own lunch too, sometimes. Occasionally her mum would leave her out something she had cooked, but usually it was all down to her. She wished her grandparents were still alive, but they had all died. Since it was the school holidays, she sometimes went to go and eat with a girlfriend. As for Matías, other than those few weird words he'd spoken outside the attic, he completely ignored her.

In any case, holidays were coming to an end. It was nearly time to start back at school.

Three
The floating cube

Heavy grey clouds drifted across the night sky. The summer temperatures had not yet dropped and Martina lay in bed reading, half covered by a sheet. Her mum had not long headed to bed.

Martina set the book down on her bedside table. She turned out the light and was about to go to sleep when she saw it. At first she thought it was a trick of her imagination. She rubbed her eyes and looked again. It was still there. Martina kneeled on the bed. It was impossible, and yet . . . Her cube – the golden cube she had found, the very same one that she dusted every week – was *floating*.

A few beams of light crept in at the window and gleamed on the gently curved edges of the cube, like the edges of a die. Her eyes were not deceiving her. It was suspended two or three centimetres above the surface of the wooden table. Unsure what to do, and still not entirely convinced, Martina took the book she had been reading and pushed it along the table, between the cube and the tabletop. It slid through seamlessly.

Martina let go of the book, which fell and ended up between the bed and the table, and she moved away from the cube, looking at it from a slightly more cautious distance. She ought to wake her mum up. Straightaway. She had to. That much was clear. And it would have been easy to do so, but something stopped her. Martina didn't quite know what that thing was, or why she followed that mysterious inner voice. But nor did she question any of it. All she did was absorb the moment.

The cube remained stationary, as if it was waiting for something. Martina glanced towards the alarm clock, which read two minutes to midnight. She took a deep breath, bit her nail for a second and finally stretched out her right hand. After what seemed like a long time, she placed it on the cube. It felt a little cooler than usual, but other than that, nothing was out of the ordinary.

Come to think of it, how often had she touched it since she'd found it? It was difficult to recall. Of course, she remembered holding it at least that first time, and surely she must've moved it around now and then. Even if it was just to dust the bedside table. Right? She didn't have specific memories but she still had the distinct feeling that it was now cooler.

On an impulse, she pushed it down. The space between the cube and the table disappeared. She let the cube go again. Her handprint remained on the upper face, like a ghost, before it faded. For a second nothing happened, and then the cube calmly lifted until it was floating in mid-air once again.

Martina took another deep breath, reached out towards the cube and closed her fingers round it. She cleared her throat and picked it up. Despite the fact it was floating, it still weighed the same as before – it was solid. Martina observed her blurred reflection on one of the faces. It was her. But at the same time, it was not.

She lay the cube on her hand to see if it would float from there. It remained flat on her palm, like an obedient pet. *Now what?* she wondered. She grimaced. She felt a burning sensation between her shoulder blades, a bite, or a sting perhaps. But she was so absorbed in the cube that she ignored it. She climbed out of bed and sat cross-legged on the wooden floor. She placed the cube on the ground.

Just like before, within seconds the cube lifted itself slowly off the floor until it was suspended a few centimetres from the surface. Martina wondered how long it had been floating without her even realizing. And what was this cube doing in her grandmother's house? What was it used for?

She picked it up again and looked at it closely. The edges connecting the flat faces were slightly round. The thing definitely looked like an enormous die. Out of pure curiosity, she touched one of the smooth edges. A pleasant fizz of electricity ran up her hand, catching her by surprise. Martina instinctively removed the finger, but after a few seconds decided to give it another go. After all, the sensation had been reasonably nice. So Martina placed her finger once more on the edge and waited to see what would happen. The soft energy flowed through her again. It felt natural to move her finger and Martina began sliding the tip of her index finger along the edge and she received a bit more of this energy. The edge seemed to light up, taking on a slightly more intense golden glow, as if her finger were, somehow, activating, even waking up that part of the cube.

She contemplated the kindled edge with a concentrated fascination and made up her mind to repeat the process with the rest of the edges. It was easy to tell where she had not yet touched. She stroked the final edge and lay the cube on the palm of her hand again. Two of the side faces began to open and dropped down, like the covers of a book.

Martina let out a small yelp and dropped the cube, which, instead of falling, gently sank, little by little, until it hung two centimetres above the floor. The upper face lifted up towards her and the whole cube opened out, the faces extending to form a flat shape like a mini hopscotch pattern.

The central face had a miniature pyramid on it. *This* was what the cube contained? As for the rest, the faces were quite thick, made from the same material both inside and out. Martina was torn between running away and getting closer. Caught between these two forces, she couldn't do either. All she could do was clench her fists.

Gradually, timid blue rays of light appeared above the tiny pyramid. At first they appeared like sparks, reaching out only around ten centimetres, but then the blue light spread above the cube like a fan until it formed a wall that reached the ceiling. It was impossible to see through it. Martina stood up and took a closer look. All she could see was a deep blue colour, something liquid. She swallowed. She studied the light at one edge and noticed that it was barely thicker than a sheet of paper. Looking through from the other side, there seemed to be nothing there at all. She could clearly see her bedroom door, the door to her mum's room and a section of the stairs.

Her mum. She ought to tell her mum. Right now. Without wasting a single second more. And yet Martina made no move towards the other bedroom. Instead, she retraced her steps, facing the blue once again. It was gorgeous, really. *I'm not scared,* she thought. This realization surprised her. Taking a deep breath, she reached out her left hand, brought it down, then lifted it again until her fingers almost grazed the light. She gave a little push. She felt no real resistance. Her hand crossed the wall of blue light and disappeared into it.

It felt fresh, like whatever was behind the light was humid. She took her hand out of the light. It seemed fine. Complete. Five fingers. One palm. Five nails. She sank it once more into the light, then reached in with her other hand, too. They both now disappeared behind the light. *It's as though I have no hands*, she said to herself, smiling.

Really? Are you smiling? Are you sure about this?

The rest happened quickly: she took another step, plunging her arms into the light, like it was a game, but then something pulled her in. A split-second later, she had disappeared into the blue light, which swallowed her completely.

Four
Novrogod

The immediate sensation was one of being surrounded by water. As if she had dived in, but without the impact on entry. One second she was in her bedroom, the next she was completely submerged.

Her vision was blurred: all she could see was dark blue. She found it hard to orient herself; she was twisting and turning around herself, going nowhere. She had no idea which way was up and which way was down. Everything seemed to lose clarity. But despite the confusion, it was also beautiful. The dark colours blended and merged together. Martina stopped fighting and let herself be carried. She moved her legs and hands and noticed the pleasant resistance of the water.

She turned her head and everything continued to be blurry, except for some bubbles that escaped from her nose and disappeared. Then she realized the obvious: her body needed more oxygen. Her heart thundered in her chest. Air. She needed to breathe. She wasn't swimming; she was drowning. She needed to come up, but the problem was she didn't know where she was, or where the 'entrance' to this ocean was located.

For a second she froze, with no clue where to go. What if she swam downwards by accident? The more panicked she felt about the lack of air, the more frantic she became. There must be some way to orientate herself. Something. Then she remembered the bubbles: air always travels to the surface.

Martina breathed out the last mouthful of air she had left. The bubbles floated upward. She kicked her legs hard, using her hands to gain momentum. *Think of the water as a rope that you're pulling yourself along,* her swimming teacher used to say as they were practising a stroke. *Squeeze your fingers together so the water can't get through*.

Her lungs were about to burst and her throat hurt – the lack of air was burning. Just when she thought she wouldn't make it, instead of dark water, she saw the night sky above her. Grey clouds scuttled across the sky like scorpions, pushed along by the wind. The waning moon cast a dim light.

Martina splashed about on the surface, coughing. She inhaled. The air smelled good, but there was a strong wind blowing that made her cold. She wiped the water from her face. A mass of yellowed leaves floated nearby, like a moving rug. Some of them stuck in her hair. She looked around and spotted the shoreline. She was in a river.

Whaaaat? she thought, but there wasn't much time to dwell on that realization. She had to get out of the water and so she focused on that.

On one edge of the river she saw a beach, with small bonfires that seemed to emerge from the sand itself, and several people. Martina waved, but it was unnecessary. A boat came straight for her and a pair of strong arms lifted her out of the water and carried her on board.

Once she was on the small deck Martina lay on her back, dripping. Her ribcage rose and fell rhythmically as her body took in air. She felt the boat turn and heard the splashing of oars. She sat up. Two men in their thirties were transporting her. One of them looked at her kindly. He had a rounded face and a shaved head. There was a red mark under his right eye. Martina presumed it was a birthmark. The other man had long hair and a dark expression in his eyes, which did not wander from his oar and the river. His features were hard and serious.

'Thank you,' Martina said to them. She didn't really know what else to say. Not under those circumstances. Were these men enemies? Saviours? They had rescued her, obviously, but something about the whole situation made her want to be cautious. At least a little.

The long-haired man remained quiet. An earring sparkled in the moonlight. The wind blew and Martina felt cold. The one with the friendly face smiled.

'Thanks for what?' he asked her.

'For saving me, of course.'

'We saved you? When?'

'Just now.'

The speaker frowned. He ran a hand over his almost non-existent hair. 'Us? Save you?'

Martina didn't reply. As the seconds passed, she was feeling more . . . well . . . poised than expected. She was alert, but not alarmed. She *was* being rescued, after all. That had to be a good thing. True, there was nothing familiar about what was happening to her . . . yet it felt somehow . . . not completely *un*natural.

Martina looked towards the beach. There were around a hundred people – men, women and children. They seemed to be waiting for her. *Waiting? For her?* She looked at them with apprehension. She was still breathing heavily, so Martina tried to calm down. Should she run away? But where to, exactly? She forced herself to adapt to the new situation. She was good at that, adapting. She'd been doing it for the last couple of months, after all.

She looked around once more. Not even the children were moving. Although Martina knew none of what was happening was normal, she thought she was simply witnessing some special occasion. She felt for the boat. It was made of hard, smooth wood.

The long-haired man climbed off the boat, up to his waist in the water. The other man clambered out too and the boat hit the sand. Martina didn't know what to do. A girl her age, around twelve or thirteen, stepped forward. She was wearing a simple white dress and was barefoot. Her chestnut-coloured curls cascaded to her waist. She had coffee-coloured eyes, a broad forehead, a firm gaze, and a smile unlike any that Martina had ever seen before.

'Welcome,' she said. 'My name is Emelia. We have been waiting for you. For a long time.'

There were no more explanations. *That's it?* thought Martina. A hundred questions arose within her, all of them mixing with one another, threatening to engulf her, but she never had the chance to utter them. Hands helped her out of the boat, and someone covered her with a shawl. Everyone stared at her: girls and boys, not blinking an eyelid, the adults gazing upon her with a certain reverence. The bonfires that had seemed to emerge from the beach were no more than holes dug in the sand with lit candles in them. The wind whipped up a few dry leaves, flying them towards the river.

On one side were swords and leather shields with sheets of iron attached by rusty nails. The shields showed signs of battle, and bite marks. The swords, with worn hilts, rested in deceitful peace beneath the tiny moon.

Emelia took Martina by the arm and guided her towards a cluster of tall trees with thick trunks. Martina felt incapable of resisting, unexpectedly at ease despite how strange everything seemed. Enormous ash trees were dotted among the biggest walnut and pine trees that Martina had ever seen. There were chestnut trees, too, with vast branches that climbed beyond the line of sight, and pink flowers shivering in the wind.

'We have been waiting for you for many moons,' said Emelia.

'Many moons?' Martina asked.

Really? Martina told herself. *Is that the best question you can come up with?*

'Of course. You don't think we are here by accident, do you? It was written that you would arrive from the River of Dark Waters under a crescent moon and that we should be there to welcome you. And so it has happened. The Prophecy has become reality.'

'What prophecy?' asked Martina, her unease growing.

'The Prophecy that stated that The Sent One would come.'

'The Sent One?'

'Of course,' replied Emelia with a smile. 'You.'

Martina opened her mouth to reply but no words came out.

'What is it?' asked Emelia.

Martina licked her lips. 'I think there's been a mistake. My name is Martina Adler.'

'*Martinadler*. I like that.'

'No, no. My first name is Martina. Adler is my surname.'

'Surname? What is that?'

'My, erm . . . It's my family name.'

'So your name is Martina?'

'Yes.'

'It's good that you are here, Martina.'

A narrow path led into the depths of the forest. It was barely wide enough for three or four people. Emelia led Martina towards it. The crowd followed them but halted when they saw that Martina and Emelia had stopped.

Emelia turned to Martina and gave her such a serene smile that Martina was almost willing to believe that this whole world fitted into a cube.

'Today, with your arrival, peace and harmony will begin in Novrogod,' Emelia said.

Martina opened her mouth to speak, but she didn't know what to say. *I have to escape from these people*, she thought. *I have to do this now.* But where would she go, exactly? Where *could* she go? And how would those people react? She didn't want to make them angry. Odd as it may seem, she didn't feel she was in any imminent danger. However, she should take it little by little. Play along for a bit. They were clearly taking her somewhere. But not as a prisoner. More like a guest.

'Where are we going?' she finally asked.

'To the village. This way. Come.'

They started walking down the path. Roots ran along the edges, occasionally crossing it like tentacles. The rustling leaves covered the sky. The crowd followed them, and several men scoured every centimetre of the darkness, seemingly on high alert.

Five
The flaming arrow

After they had walked perhaps two hundred metres, maybe even less, a wall of bound-together sharp wooden spikes rose up out of nowhere. Two reinforced doors creaked open. Inside were around thirty huts made from mud and stone, topped with straw roofs held up by wooden posts. The moving crowd looked towards the centre of the village, where there was a clearing. It was set with a large circular table covered with white cloths. Off to one side, some people were roasting meats, while salads lay already prepared on a table nearby.

There were around fifty people in the village when Martina, Emelia and the group from the river arrived. When the villagers saw Martina they let out a collective gasp of astonishment. Emelia smiled.

'Martina,' she said in a low voice. 'Welcome to the Village of the Crescent Moon.' She then addressed those watching in a louder voice: 'This is Martina.'

An old man with hair and a beard that were completely white took a few steps forward. He was the only one to move. He was fat with a round face, not much taller than Martina herself. His eyes shone and his arms hung comfortably by his sides. He was wearing a long blue toga over a pair of trousers and his feet were squeezed into leather shoes.

'Princess. Is it true?'

Princess?! said Martina's voice in her head. *Princess? Who are they calling* princess?

Emelia walked over to the old man, took his hand and beamed one of her incredible smiles at him.

'Yes, Glido.'

'You saw her emerge from the River of Dark Waters?'

'With my own eyes.'

The old man swallowed and looked at Martina.

'We all saw it, Glido,' said Emelia.

'So . . . the Prophecy . . .' stammered Glido.

Martina could contain herself no longer. 'Sorry to butt in, but –'

Glido let out a huge guffaw, interrupting Martina mid-sentence. He arched his back and threw his hands up into the air. His laughter rose up over the wall of wooden spikes that protected the Village of the Crescent Moon and was lost in the forest, rising up towards the sky.

'Finally! The Sent One has arrived!' he announced.

And without waiting a moment longer, he marched over to Martina and embraced her in a hug so tight Martina could swear she felt her bones creak. The village broke into joyful cries and laughter.

'Peace, harmony and hope are among us,' said Glido as he released Martina.

'Erm, I think there's some sort of confusion . . .' Martina said to Emelia, who was watching.

'Of course there's some confusion!' exclaimed Glido. 'Not just some, but a whole heap of confusion! We have a guest, and we are yet to offer her anything to eat! Where are our manners?!'

From some metal pots came a delicious aroma that mingled with the smell of the roasting meats, the juices of which ran off into the fire as the fat sizzled. Martina could also smell freshly baked bread and see the table of salads. She suddenly felt ravenous.

'No, you don't understand. There's a problem . . .' Martina tried to say.

'Just one? Thousands!' answered Glido. 'But none of them will be resolved on an empty stomach. Let's eat! Music! Today is a celebration!'

Then he walked away. The only person who remained standing by her side was Emelia. *Princess Emelia,* Martina reminded herself. Emelia smiled at her and shrugged.

Martina ate and drank until she was fit to burst. After all, why not? She forgot the issue of whether or not she was The Sent One. The villagers treated her in a special way, and she allowed herself to be carried along by it, content. After the food came dancing. Martina had the best night in a long time, without thinking about anything – no divorced parents, new homes, future schools or attic bedrooms. In a way, this . . . event . . . happening to her – whatever it was – seemed like the most right thing ever. Perhaps it was a dream, the best virtual reality game in history or quantum physics gone crazy, but she made an effort not to think too much about it. She realized it had been a long time since she had had any simple, mind-blowing fun.

At one point she went to sit down to take a rest from the dancing and looked over towards Emelia. She saw her sitting next to a shadow. She walked over to them. The shadow was a boy with brown hair, no older than five years old. He was tossing and turning in his sleep, crying out.

'Hi,' said Emelia as Martina approached.

'Hi.'

Martina sat down next to them. The boy's hair was damp and stuck to his forehead.

'What's wrong with him?'

'He's sick.'

'Will he get better?'

'Of course. But now we no longer have any Wizardry, his body will have to fight the illness on its own.'

'Any what?'

'Wizardry. Voraz stole it, as you know.'

'Voraz?'

'Of course. That's why you're here, isn't it?'

Martina stayed silent. She didn't know what to say. Emelia brushed the boy's hair out of his face as he wriggled in his sleep.

'If we had Wizardry, we would not have had such

problems, but now . . .' Emelia sighed and stood up. 'Let's take a walk.'

As they headed away from the party, leaving the sick boy under someone else's care, Martina thought about how strange all this was and yet how easily she had fitted in. However, sooner or later they would realize that she was not The Sent One. She wondered what would happen then.

None of the alternatives that came to mind seemed all that appealing. She needed to get back home. That was the wisest course of action. Before things got out of hand. She had been simply letting things happen, allowing herself to be dragged into some kind of game, but she had to deal with the fact that this wasn't a game for all these people. Whoever they were expecting, it wasn't her.

'Look,' she began. 'I'm sorry I got carried away, but I need to get back.'

'Get back? To where?'

'To my . . . house.'

To my life, she was about to add, but it sounded a bit dramatic, like she was overreacting. *Am I, though?* Martina asked herself. Probably not. Wasn't everything that was happening enough to rattle anyone? Or at least make them nervous?

Yes.

And still she felt an odd sense of comfort. A *small* sense of comfort, true, but . . .

Emelia flashed a smile. 'Which is where . . .? Your house, I mean.'

'Well . . . Look, the thing is, I've never been here . . .'

'We know. And we know you are supposed to be a little confused. Or we knew that was a possibility, at least. But don't worry, everything will sort itself out. You're here and that's all that matters.'

Part of the difficulty, thought Martina, was how everybody made everything sound so easy, as if nothing unusual was happening.

'OK . . . see, um, that's the thing: I don't think anything is going to just sort itself out – and I really need to get going . . .'

Just as Martina and Emelia moved away from the clearing, an enormous spotty dog with a long muzzle and bright eyes trotted towards them. It looked large, and as it approached them its head was lowered and its ears flapped. Its fur was short and dense. Martina watched it and felt her heart beating quickly in her chest – the dog came up to her waist and if it was angry, it could devour her in just a few quick mouthfuls.

'Socrates . . .?' said Emelia.

The dog continued its beeline straight towards Martina. Instinctively, Martina stopped and when the dog reached her, she took a couple of steps backwards.

'Socrates . . .?' repeated Emelia.

But Socrates ignored her completely and sniffed the recent arrival. He sniffed her feet and then followed his nose up to her knees. After a few seconds – during which Martina feared the loss of her leg – Socrates began to wag his tail and licked one of her feet. His wet tongue tickled and Martina tried not to laugh.

'I think Socrates approves,' remarked Emelia, smiling.

As if to demonstrate just how true these words were, Socrates put his forepaws up on to Martina's chest. Standing up like this, he was the same height as Martina. The blow was so forceful that Martina had to grasp Socrates' legs to stop herself from toppling backwards. The dog took this as a sign of friendship and began to lick her face.

'Socrates, eh,' said Martina. 'Like the philosopher?'

'Philosopher?'

'Yes. Socrates. The Greek philosopher.'

'Socrates was a great Wizard.'

'No, he was a philosopher. In Greece.'

'Greece? I have never heard of that village.'

'What do you mean? Greece. In Europe. Socrates lived in Athens, the capital of Greece, in the times before Jesus.'

'Before whom?'

'Jesus,' replied Martina, in a low voice.

Emelia fell silent. The sound of music, voices and the murmur of the River of Dark Waters reached them.

'I don't know anyone called that. And I have never heard of Greece,' said Emelia.

'It's a country.'

'What's a country? We don't have those here in Novrogod. Socrates was Novrogod's first Wizard to pit himself against Voraz and defeat him. We have him to thank for all this peace, harmony and hope after so many years of darkness. Socrates has been dead for a long time, and we named this pup in his memory. But now that Voraz is back . . .'

'What do you mean he's back? Back from where?' Martina asked.

'He was defeated and died, supposedly. Now, he's returned.'

'Like, from the dead?' Martina said with a chuckle.

'Well . . . I'm not sure. All we know is that he's at work again.'

'At work?' Martina realized she was acting a bit like a parrot, but she was feeling uneasy at this turn in the conversation and couldn't help herself.

'Yes,' continued Emelia. 'Gaining control of the Wizardry that surrounds us here.'

'Sorry, wizardry?' *Please, Martina, stop it. Control yourself.*

'Sure – the energy that binds us all, that keeps everything together. The energy of life. But now, with your arrival, his days are numbered,' finished Emelia with a smile.

A loud whistling sound cut through the air, interrupting their conversation. The joy drained from Emelia's face. Socrates put his feet on the ground once more. In the darkness of the night, an intense orange stain crossed the sky and embedded itself in one of the straw roofs. An arrow with a flaming tip. An arrow on fire.

A grey, hazy smoke began to rise, reminding Martina of the mist that surrounded the Wanderer in the Darkness – that hooded figure who inhabited her dreams.

Six
Escape

The flames that rose from the rooftop were reflected in Emelia's pupils. The straw and wooden beams were burning. Socrates was the only one of the three to react, whimpering in fear. Then a shower of arrows rained on to the village, their orangey-yellow tips leaving a blazing trail as they crossed the sky.

Emelia turned pale and stumbled a few steps towards the village. The air now smelled of smoke. Martina looked at her new friend, unsure what to do. Even more arrows fell on the huts. Screams filled the air. Some came from inside the village, but others came from outside. More than screams – they were high-pitched, indecipherable shrieks.

'Tugs,' muttered Emelia to herself.

'Tugs . . .?' asked Martina.

Emelia turned to her as if suddenly snapping out of a trance. She was ashen, her lips were pressed into a thin line and her eyes had darkened. The atmosphere had turned grey and it was hard to see. The smell of burning filled Martina's nostrils and the smoke caused a choking sensation in her throat.

'They mustn't find you here,' murmured Emelia.

'*Who* mustn't find me here?'

'Them.'

The fact that Emelia didn't really answer the question only made Martina more apprehensive. *Them. Who's them?* she wondered. She dared not ask.

'Why not?'

'They'd try to kill you. Or worse.'

'Worse?!'

Fortunately – or not – the answer never came. The shrieks that had erupted from outside the fence had silenced the villagers, and through the murky air Martina could make out ghostly shadows, unrecognizable from a distance, the smoke and ash clouding her vision. The shapes climbed the fence and entered the village. Their movements were quick and agile, and Martina could hear the shrieks more clearly. The earth vibrated with their footsteps.

'What's happening?' Martina asked.

'Voraz's army. He must have worked out I'm here. You have to hide. Now,' replied Emelia.

Socrates barked towards the tugs. They were supple, swift creatures, like monkeys, but two metres tall, running towards the village. Martina coughed and felt her eyes streaming.

'Wha–?' she asked.

But Emelia was striding towards the clearing. The first sound of clashes of swords and shields reached Martina's ears. She also felt that tingling sensation again, the same one she had had when Nicole had grabbed her hair. Right at the back of her neck. Where her birthmark was. Only this time, the sensation was more intense.

'The river,' interrupted Emelia. 'They won't find you there. It's me they're looking for.'

Martina tried to ignore the tingling on her neck and focus on what was going on. The tingling – almost obediently – waned.

'There's a black stake in the fence over there. It's a disguised door,' Emelia said. She stopped, turned to Martina and took hold of her hands. 'You are here and that is what matters. The fate of Novrogod is in your hands.'

Martina stood watching her, not knowing how to respond or what to do. *In my hands? Nothing is ever in my hands. Not really. And if it were, it'd probably not end well.*

And, above all, it was hard to understand exactly what was going on. She would have to play it by ear.

'Look –' Martina began.

'Socrates, look after her,' Emelia said, cutting her off.

Emelia ran towards the clearing, leaving Martina alone. A terrible fear washed over her. It felt like vertigo, the sensation of falling but never hitting the ground. Yet she also felt as if her feet were nailed to the ground and she couldn't move, however anxious she was to get out of there. Panic finally took over and she ran. The huts flashed by, and she searched for the blackened stake in the fence. It wasn't hard to find. She pushed and it gave way, revealing a space just large enough for her to pass through. She scurried through it and raced back along the path towards the beach by the river where she had arrived. She stopped and glanced behind her: fire and smoke. Her only companion now was Socrates. The dog wagged its tail and sat down. Martina swallowed and turned to the river. She couldn't stay there. *And anyway, I have to get up at seven to go to school,* she thought, almost breaking into hysterical laughter. And it wasn't just school that was waiting for her. There were also her parents, old friends. Even step siblings. A whole world.

This is completely insane.

Martina sank one foot into the water. It was cold. Socrates whimpered. Martina waded out further into the river. *What happens if I drown?* The thought ran through her mind, but she batted it away. Somehow she felt certain that she wouldn't. She didn't know why, but she was sure.

The water reached her waist and surged against her. She took a few more steps before plunging herself fully into the river. She couldn't see anything, but she kicked and moved her arms. She swam like she had done before, just in the opposite direction. Her throat was tight, but she didn't feel like she was lacking air. She swam down until she saw a rectangular light, soft and silvery, distorted by the movement of the water.

Remaining calm, Martina swam towards it. The light was utterly resplendent, even under the water. She stretched her hands out in front of her and felt resistance against her palms. It felt like she was pushing against the fabric of a nylon bag, but much, much finer. Martina kicked her legs and pushed. The membrane stretched before it snapped over her fingers.

She felt fresh air on her fingertips. She pushed, her face now pressing against the membrane before breaking through. More fresh air. Martina filled her lungs and opened her eyes wide.

She couldn't believe what she was seeing.

It was the living room in her own home. It couldn't be, but it was. There were the sofas, the doorway, the library her mum had set up. She kicked her legs. It was like emerging head first from a well. She positioned her arms on the edges of the opening and heaved. The rest of her body slid through, and she tumbled on to the floor.

She looked up and turned to see where she'd come from. Her own frightened image stared back at her from Grandma Famke's old mirror. That's where she'd popped out. And that wasn't all. Martina looked down at her body. It was dry, completely dry.

Breathing heavily, she raced up the stairs and returned to her bedroom. The lamp was still on and the golden cube was lying on the floor, closed. Martina looked at the time on her clock: midnight exactly. Only two minutes had passed since she'd last looked at it, when the cube had opened and . . .

It can't be. That's simply not possible.

But sitting there in her bedroom, Martina couldn't find any plausible answer.

'That was one of the weirdest dreams I have ever had,' she said out loud, as if to convince herself. But even then, she didn't fully believe it. Could she be dreaming? Yes, perhaps . . . If that was the case, it was a very, very strange dream.

Yes, and now as well as having weird dreams, you've started sleepwalking too, she thought.

Or maybe she was simply telling herself whatever was necessary to calm her fears.

Seven
Classes

Martina's alarm went off at seven o'clock, dragging her from her sleep. The memory of Novrogod was lost among the haze of her dreams. Martina checked the cube. It was sitting innocently on her bedside table. Had it really been floating? Surely not. In broad daylight, to even imagine so felt like an absurd idea. And yet, she still had doubts. It was a slightly uncomfortable feeling. Something she could not put her finger on. She briefly pondered on it. The problem was, what could it have been aside from a dream?

Martina dressed in a blue skirt, a white shirt, a blue and red tie, and her black school shoes. Then she grabbed her breakfast and headed off for the first day at her new school. It was the same school that Matías and Nicole attended – worse luck – and her father had insisted she go too. It wasn't far away, and it had a good reputation, so her mother had agreed.

A huge number of pupils descended on the playing field in front of the school. At the far side was a low wall topped with a decorative metal railing and beyond that the large school yard. As Martina walked around the field she could hear the voices of friends greeting each other after the holidays. She felt like she was being swept up in a tidal wave, yet no one seemed to notice her. Today, though, she preferred it that way. The first person she saw was Matías. He was looking smart in his uniform and Martina felt a pang of joy, just from spotting a familiar face, but it soon faded away. It wasn't like they were friends or anything. Matías was with his friends and didn't appear to have even recognized her. Two girls about Matías's age linked arms with him, one on each side, and they walked away giggling.

If Matías was there, Nicole must be there too. Martina looked around, trying to locate her, but she couldn't see her anywhere. She went through the metal gate and walked across the concrete yard that ran up to the building itself. Suddenly her right leg was tripped and someone gave her a hard shove. Martina landed on the ground.

A sea of faces turned towards her. Her knees and hands burned, but she quickly stood up. There was Nicole, a smirk plastered to her face.

'Oops, did you trip?' she said as she flounced past.

Next to her walked a girl who was the perfect replica of Nicole, tall with an angelic face and long, straight blonde hair. Martina, of course, had never seen the girl before and didn't know her name, but she spoke with the same dismissive tone as Nicole.

'Yeah. You should be careful, *Ketchup*.'

'Why ketchup?' Martina asked foolishly.

'Cos it looks like you sprayed your head with it, ha!' the girl replied.

Martina watched the pair walk away. The two of them smiled and the rest of the pupils seemed to smile with them. She hadn't said a single word to anybody and yet already she had a nickname. The only person who did not smile was Matías. He watched in silence, his face serious, as if to say, *Go to your classroom. Go now.*

Dear Diary,

Today I finished my first week at Stevenson. The school isn't too bad but it's really big, with kids from pre-school right up to teenagers. The buildings are four storeys high – the classrooms start on the first floor with the hall and canteen below. The walls are all covered in pictures, photos and phrases created by the students. There are three form groups. Most of the kids have been there since they were little, so they've put all of us 'new starters' together in the same class. One of the other new girls seems nice. She doesn't know anyone either. Her name's Clara and we sometimes sit together and talk.

I still miss my old school though. Nearly every day I call or message Gabriela, Magdalena, Mariana and Stefanía. Even Paco wrote to me one day to see how I'm getting on.

Nicole goes to Stevenson as well and her best friend is a girl called Nadine. They just love trying to make my life hell, so I've mostly been staying in the classroom at break times. They can't get me in there. They both look in from outside and laugh, but I focus on some work or do some reading. I only go outside when the teachers tell me I shouldn't be in there on my own, or when I see Nicole and Nadine are busy doing something else. I just don't understand why Nadine hates me so much.

The teachers give us so much homework, but at least it's something to do. Mum is almost always out at the Embassy or working on a translation at home. All I hear of her is the computer keys going tap tap tap.

Whenever I wake up or go to bed, I look at Grandma's cube to see if it's floating. It is ridiculous, yeah, but, still, I just can't stop myself. I know all that stuff about being The Sent One was just a dream, or something like that, but . . . it felt so real. And it lasted so long. I thought about telling someone about it all. My new friend Clara, perhaps. I don't know. It feels silly, or weird, to talk about your dreams. Right? Or is it OK to do that? Anyway, it'd be fun to have another dream like that, but I keep waking up during the night. I think I'm scared now of sleepwalking around the house.

The weekend was approaching. It was time for Martina to go to her dad's and she wasn't particularly looking forward to it. Not because she didn't want to see him, but because it meant staying at his house, and that meant being near to Nicole. Matías was there, too, of course, but he tended to keep his distance. And he was hard to figure out, most of the time. He made her curious, true, but there was no way to explore that curiosity. He didn't seem to be interested in her, but that was fine.

When Martina arrived with her backpack full of clothes and a copy of the book *The Master of Ballantrae* by Robert Louis Stevenson, Nadine was there too, doing her homework with Nicole. Matías was out and Martina's dad was working late. When Matías walked in some time later, the girls and Nicole's mum were all watching a film. Nadine's face lit up.

'Hi Matías,' she cooed in a sickly-sweet voice that turned Martina's stomach. Nadine smiled and Martina could see the yellow chewing gum going around and around in her mouth. Matías glanced briefly in Nadine's direction, as if looking at nothing more than a hole in the sofa, before turning to Martina.

'Ah, Martina, I thought you might be here. How are you?' he asked.

She looked at him in surprise.

'Erm . . . F-fine,' she replied. 'You?'

'Fantastic, thanks.'

Matías briefly smiled at her and, without waiting for any further response, he walked back out of the room again.

'You're welcome . . .' murmured Martina, disappointed that he was leaving already. It would've been nice to talk some more. Matías didn't seem to hear.

'Shh!' hissed Nadine, her eyes ablaze. 'If you hadn't noticed, Ketchup, we're watching a film.'

Silvia turned towards Nadine, absorbed in the film.

'What's that? You want some ketchup?' She waved a hand. 'On its own?'

'Oh, no thanks. I don't eat it like that any more. Now I mainly eat it just with fideos.'

'Oh, OK,' replied Silvia.

Nadine's eyes turned back to the TV screen. Martina knew Nadine wouldn't let this go, but right there and then, she really didn't care. Nadine would always be involved in her little wars; it was best to ignore her. The same was true of Nicole.

Martina watched the rest of the film with the others, but her mind was elsewhere and she found it hard to follow the story. Instead, she thought about school, the sudden but fleeting, inconsequential moments when Matías addressed her, and that dream about Novrogod. She didn't think dreams had a hidden meaning or anything like that, to be honest. They were just a jumble of chaotic thoughts. But she relished the details, such as the name of the place: Novrogod. It was an unusual word that would stick in your memory, and she was sure she had never heard it before.

School usually started early and pupils worked through until two o'clock, when they went home for lunch. On

Tuesdays and Wednesdays, however, Martina had an extra two-hour Portuguese lesson after school. The pupils were given half an hour's break before the class, and everyone brought a packed lunch and sat on the grass to eat.

That particular Tuesday, Martina was just sitting down with Clara when two shadows crept over her. A pair of hands reached over and grabbed her lunchbox. Martina looked up. The figures were silhouetted against the bright sun, but she easily recognized the cascading manes of hair.

'Mmm. Chicken and rice,' said Nadine, sniffing the food. 'Thank you very much.'

'Hey, give me back my lunch.'

Martina went to stand up, but Nadine gave her a shove. Martina toppled backwards. Nadine took a few steps forward, her shadow completely engulfing Martina on the ground.

'Or what? You gonna come and get it?'

Martina looked around her. Clara had shuffled away slightly. Everyone else was watching, the same message visible in their eyes: *I'm staying out of this.* Nobody was going to help her. She was on her own.

'Martina,' said Nadine. 'We don't want to hurt you. In fact, quite the opposite. Think of us as your guardians. We'll make sure nobody nicks your lunch, and in return all we ask is that you give us a little bit of what we're protecting, right? That way we can make sure nobody's going to steal it from you.' Nadine and Nicole grinned as Martina watched them in silence. She sat on the ground and straightened her clothes the best she could.

'What happened?' asked Martina, standing up. 'Don't they feed you at home?'

'Actually, no. They give me money to buy whatever I like for lunch, but now it seems I can get it for free, so I'll be able to save my money for something better!'

Nadine beamed at her, but Martina stayed silent. She had no idea what to do or say; she couldn't fight them both. When Nadine realized Martina had no intention of doing anything she took a couple of steps away.

'Thanks for the lunch,' she said, and strode off with Nicole.

Martina folded her arms. Apparently, Nicole and Nadine's little wars were not that little, after all. *Don't cry,* was all she could think. *Don't cry.*

Clara now came over to her.

'Here. I've got enough for two.'

'No, it's fine. I'm not hungry.'

'Come on, my mum always gives me enough to feed an army and if I don't go home with an empty tub, she starts going on about it.'

Martina ate some of Clara's *milanesa* with potato puree without really tasting it. She was going to have to do *something*. Her only option was to eat at school and she didn't want to skip two meals a week. Worse, she only had one day before she would next see Nadine or Nicole at lunchtime.

But by then, everything would have changed.

Eight
The Mark of Light

Maybe it was simply coincidence, but that very afternoon, after she'd got home from school, the cube popped into Martina's mind. It was still sitting in its usual place by her bed. She picked it up. It weighed exactly the same as before, and however much she poked and prodded it, she could not get it to open. That was to be expected, of course. The same thing had happened on the other couple of times she had grabbed the cube after she'd had the dream. It seemed – it was – completely and utterly solid.

She finished her biology project on cells and nodded off after reading only a couple of pages of *The Master of Ballantrae*. Her mum was working late at the Embassy so she could doze in peace.

She curled up in her favourite position, on her side facing the wall. She slept deeply, yet through the haze she felt her mother's fingers stroking the hair at the nape of her neck.

'Mum, I'm asleep . . .'

'There it is. The Mark,' replied a man's voice.

Martina's eyes snapped open. She bolted upright in bed and spun round. A man with broad shoulders and greying hair tied back with a ribbon was staring at her, his eyes unreadable. His tall body was enveloped in a blue toga, trousers and leather boots. 'Of course you're The Sent One. You have the Mark of Light, the shape of the sun, on your neck.'

Just as Martina went to scream, she jerked awake. She was still in bed, panting for breath, her body covered in a film of sweat. She checked behind her; she was alone. She sighed with relief but she could still feel those fingers on the back of her neck.

The Sent One? That strange name again . . . Martina glanced at the cube. It looked like some innocent trinket. She scratched between her shoulders. Her skin was still prickling where the fingers had touched her. She got up, went into the bathroom and, having adjusted the angles of the mirrors on both sides, she parted her hair and looked.

Yes, there it was, her famous red birthmark. She remembered it as a shapeless blob, but what she saw now was different. The blob had changed. Now it was a defined circle with rays spreading out from it. The shape of the sun.

Martina thought about the cube once more. Had it all really been a dream? Or was it just something she told herself to keep from going crazy? What if the cube had really lifted itself up? The idea seemed preposterous, sure, but somehow not completely impossible, at least not right then.

She racked her brain, trying to understand. Whenever she looked at it, the cube was always sitting calmly on the table, but she had never checked it around midnight – the time when she saw it floating. Was that what she was supposed to do?

She went to change out of her sweat-soaked T-shirt and opened the wardrobe door. She stood there frozen to the spot. On the other side of the door, a single word had been written:

Kelytong

It was the first time Martina had ever seen the word there. *Kelytong*? What was that? Had it been there all along and she just hadn't seen it? Or had she written it while she was sleepwalking?

Her thoughts returned to the cube. She felt on the verge of something, like she was standing on the edge of a trampoline, just about to jump . . . only not into a pool, full of water, but into something unknown.

Was she ready for it? Ready for something she basically knew nothing about? It was hard to tell – but that suddenly seemed fine. Who wanted to do only the things that they were perfectly ready for? If anything, this was the chance to discover something new, even a new Martina, one she could be but still wasn't. If there was a leap she had to take, why not? Perhaps she could try it with grace, as divers did, flying more than falling.

She glanced over at the cube and she resolved to stay up late that night. It felt ridiculous, but she wanted to be there watching it right on the stroke of midnight. Because the last time she'd seen the cube float, she'd ended up running away from that strange place, wherever and whatever that place may be.

And she'd had enough of running away. She knew that things could go wrong and that none of it made much sense. But, at the same time, she felt drawn to Novrogod by a force that was outside her, and also coming from her very core. She was going to go through with this. If the cube lifted, she was *willingly* – and perhaps unreasonably – going to take that leap.

At five minutes to midnight, Martina was in position, her grey eyes fixed on the cube. She had left no explanatory note to anyone about what she was planning to do. What could it even say? *Hey, I just walked into some blue light that comes out of a golden cube that floats at midnight and that my grandmother, whose origin is unclear, decided to leave behind, probably hoping I would find it one day. This light takes me to a place called Novrogod, which could be dangerous, but don't worry, I'll be back in time for breakf–*

Her thoughts were abruptly interrupted when, with no warning whatsoever, the cube lifted itself a couple of centimetres off the wooden tabletop. For a few seconds she didn't really breathe. How could she? Her entire body seemed to just stop altogether. All she could do was observe, watch in awe as now between the cube and the . . . well, the rest of the world . . . there was only . . . *air*.

Nothing else.

Wait a minute . . . she told herself, slowly. *I am awake now . . . I am! This is REAL.*

It was somehow a relief. A liberation. Right there and then, Martina knew her destiny was about to change. If the cube was floating, then she was about to cross over into Novrogod. She recognized this with the serenity of someone who had known all along exactly what would happen next.

Nine
The Crazy Skull

This time, when she broke through the barrier between the worlds there was only darkness in the overcast night sky and the water in the river was darker still. All was quiet and Martina found herself completely alone. She calmly swam ashore and felt the cool sand on the soles of her feet.

She removed the backpack she'd hastily packed and brought with her, and opened it. Inside, wrapped in plastic bags, was a bundle of dry clothes, shoes and a packet of biscuits. She changed out of her wet things and walked towards where the village had been. All that was left of the thatched huts were a few charred stones.

What now? she wondered. *What do I do? Where do I go?*

She sat down and took a few deep breaths, controlling her urge to run away and return to the safety of her bedroom. *Kelytong.* It had to be the key. But what was Kelytong? And where was it?

She returned to the banks of the River of Dark Waters. She looked around, trying to orientate herself. About a hundred metres downstream, the beach ended and a path led into the forest. Martina sighed and thought to herself, *It'd be far worse if there was nothing at all*. She slipped on her backpack and headed towards the path.

The silence was suffocating. It was the middle of the night. The footpath was a flat dirt track, a couple of metres wide. She followed the path for about two hours, enveloped by a tomb-like stillness, interrupted only by the gurgling river running alongside.

She was surrounded by forest. Thirty-metre-tall ash trees, oaks with broad boughs and gnarled chestnut trees buried their roots in the dark earth. Some monstrous-looking banana plants and grey-trunked sycamores completed the wall of vegetation.

Beyond the undergrowth, she could hear distant sounds. Maybe they were animal calls. Or unidentifiable whispers. She looked around uneasily on both sides of the path, but she couldn't see anything. The grey trunks and the foliage formed an impassable barricade.

She stopped still, her calf muscles tensed. What was that? Noises reached her ears and they didn't sound like they came from an animal. Voices. They were definitely voices.

She sprinted forward and a shiver ran down her neck. Slowly the voices grew louder and Martina could smell food, too. Now she heard laughter. She had a sudden flashback to her first visit to Novrogod.

A few metres further on, the path broadened out and the trees retreated to reveal a patch of bare land and a soft light. In the middle of the clearing stood a large hut, very similar to the ones in the Village of the Crescent Moon. A worn, rusty sign creaked in the wind. On it was a picture of a smiling skull and the inscription: *The Crazy Skull. Shelter and accommodation*.

It didn't look like the most appealing place, but it didn't make much sense to keep on walking, not when she was alone in the middle of nowhere. Besides, she was tired and thirsty. She took a firm step towards the door.

No sooner had she set foot inside than a deafening silence fell over the place. Martina could even hear the buzzing of a couple of blowflies. The yellow light from some candles danced shadows on the faces on the people present. The wooden floor was stained, and some filthy, poorly dressed men sat at the few tables. A counter made from tree trunks separated the kitchen from the dining room at the back, next to a staircase leading to the upstairs rooms.

Several pairs of eyes turned towards her and Martina felt her breath catch. She thought of turning tail and fleeing – something she might well have done had it not been for a large woman with a tea-towel over one shoulder, who smiled at her.

''Ello sweet'eart,' she said as she broke off from dealing with a couple of men at a nearby table so she could attend to Martina. 'Welcome to my guesthouse. My name's Bernarda. What's yours?'

'M-Martina.'

'Martina. What a beautiful name. What you doing round 'ere at this time of night, Martina?'

'Erm . . .'

'Where are your parents?'

Bernarda gave her a look of concern. Martina simply shook her head.

'They left you all alone?' asked Bernarda.

Martina shrugged.

'Sometimes I just don't understand why some parents even 'ave children. Now, you come on over here. Are you hungry? 'Ave you had some dinner?'

'I'm thirsty.'

'Very well.'

Bernarda placed one large hand on Martina's shoulder and guided her further inside. She led Martina to a table where a couple of scruffy, bearded men sat drinking.

'Off yer go. Out.'

The men tried to protest – one of them even raised one of his fingers at her – but Bernarda would not let them speak.

'I said, out!' she ordered.

The men stood up, picked up their drinks and left, leaving behind the wet circles from their glasses on the tabletop. Bernarda beamed at Martina.

'Sit here,' she said, motioning to the now empty table.

'Thanks,' replied Martina, and she sat down on the wooden bench, which was as long as the table itself.

It was odd to be treated with such deference, and

Martina didn't know exactly how to react, but it was nice to have someone to take care of her like that. It probably wasn't the best idea for her to be wandering alone at night round there, and now she was in the guesthouse she felt much safer. It was unclear how she would continue her journey – going where, exactly? – but at least she knew she had a place to stay through the night until sunrise.

'Very good. Now, let me bring you a glass of water,' Bernarda said.

And without another glance, off she went.

'What you all looking at?' she yelled at everyone else. 'You never seen a girl before? Go on, back to your chit-chat. None of that staring, all right? She's not a work of art! More wine anyone?'

More than one person said yes, and to Martina's relief they soon forgot about her. She placed her backpack down next to her, close by – even though there was plenty of space – and clasped her fingers in her lap. She looked around at The Crazy Skull's clientele.

They were all men, and not particularly hygienic ones at that. They had greasy hair, dirty like their clothes, and stubble from several days without shaving. They sat around in groups of two or three, chatting and laughing in low voices. Martina silently gave thanks for not having come across any of these guys on her journey.

Her attention was drawn to a bald man with skin as white as paper. He had his back to her and she couldn't see his face, but his sizeable neck bulged. A broad tunic covered his enormous body and traced the outline of his arms, which were ridiculously short. He was the only one eating anything, and seemed relatively harmless.

In the air hung a mixture of smells – damp, sweat and food – and Martina decided she wouldn't stay there long. As soon as it was daylight she'd be on her way. She'd go straight back home. This whole idea had been a huge mistake.

''Ere you go.' Bernarda was back, her footsteps clunking on the wooden floor. 'Some nice fresh water.'

'Thank you,' said Martina.

'You're very welcome,' answered Bernarda, then she sat down on the bench opposite Martina. The wood creaked beneath her. 'So then, tell me about you. You said your name's Martina, was that it?'

'Mm-hmm.'

'Where did you get those odd-looking clothes?'

Martina looked down at herself and realized she stood out like a sore thumb. Novrogodian clothes looked about 200 years older in terms of style than the ones she was wearing.

'It's all I have,' she replied.

'Clearly,' said Bernarda. 'Where you from?'

Martina took a sip of water.

'Far away.'

'A girl like you shouldn't be wandering 'round making long journeys alone. These lands can be dangerous.'

'I know,' said Martina. She tried to sound calm, but she was becoming more and more anxious. She finished her water and realized she had a problem.

'I have no money.'

Bernarda snorted like an elephant.

'Who does nowadays? Nobody. Accept it or go kaboom, sweet'eart, that's what I say. Don't you worry. In any case, I wouldn't go charging you for a simple glass of water, now. It's on the 'ouse!'

'Thank you.'

'Nothing to be thankful for. Us girls've got to stick together and look out for one another, eh?'

Martina smiled and nodded.

'Very good, Martina. Now, let's see.' Bernarda rested her elbows on the table and leaned forward. 'Why you travelling alone? Where you going?'

Martina licked her lips. She decided to go for it.

'Kelytong.'

'Kelytong?'

'Mm-hmm.'

'I see. You know that's still quite a long way from here, don't yer?'

So, it's a place then, thought Martina, nodding in relief. *At least someone's heard of it. Yeah, well, great. And what exactly are you going to do when you get there, big brain? It doesn't really look like you've got a super-giant plan, now, do you?*

And yet . . . it still felt right. At least in part. She had had to come; she had had to cross over to this Novrogod place – that much she knew. And she'd done it. She *was* there. She couldn't just turn around and pretend nothing had happened. Even if she'd been thinking about going back a few minutes ago, now a voice inside her urged her to keep going.

'As I said, it's dangerous for a girl like you to be travelling alone,' continued Bernarda.

Martina didn't want to come across as a completely lost cause.

'I know,' she said again.

Bernarda stuck her tongue into one of her cheeks.

'Look,' she said. 'I don't normally get involved in stuff like this – each to their own and all that – but, if you'd like, I can 'elp you out. Would that be good?'

'Of course.'

'I know some people who are leaving today and travelling to Intercesora by cart. Kelytong's on the way. If you want, you –'

'Can I go with them?' interrupted Martina.

'They're some of the few people round 'ere you can trust.'

Martina looked around the place.

'You interested?' asked Bernarda.

'Yes,' replied Martina.

'Great. Just give me a second then.'

Bernarda stood up and walked towards the counter, leaving Martina's empty glass on the side, and went to talk to two individuals who were quietly talking and drinking. One of them, short and with chubby arms, had a thick beard of a peculiar reddish colour, ending in small braids. He was completely bald and wore several earrings on two distractingly big ears. The other, with blonde hair and restless blue eyes, was taller and lankier. Below his throat, he had a tattoo that read 'real grit'.

The conversation didn't last long. Martina couldn't see their faces very well or hear the exact words, but the three were talking in a very animated way. Bernarda stood up.

The men looked over at Martina and smiled briefly at her, obliging her to return it. Bernarda came over to Martina, sat down again and put her tea-towel on the table.

'All sorted,' she said. 'Them two men over there are Aton and Svarko. They're traders who travel the length and breadth of Novrogod. I know they don't look like it, but they are trustworthy. I've known 'em a long time.'

'Thank you, Bernarda. I don't know what I would have done without your help.'

'Well, to start with, I'd like to know you got there safely. I always wanted a daughter. Life gives you wishes but don't always grant 'em.' She swung her tea-towel back over her shoulder. 'But anyway, here's me telling you my sob stories. The important thing is, you got 'ere, and you'll surely get to Kelytong.'

'Thank you. Truly.'

'Now, you listen to me. Aton and Svarko'll be leaving in a few minutes. They don't like to stop for long. It's their way of making sure they don't get robbed along the way. They don't want anyone to think they're taking you with 'em 'cause otherwise others will try to take advantage and want to hitch a ride with 'em. You know what I'm saying?'

'Of course.'

'So, anyway, you walk out of 'ere as if you're going on your way, and they'll meet you round the side. They'll be waiting for you, and they'll put you in their cart, hidden among the goods. Understood?'

'Got it.'

'Well, that's it then. Take care.'

Martina nodded. The woman smiled, stood up and left. Martina sighed. She put her backpack on and went outside.

Ten
Underway

Martina walked round the side of the building. The leaves from the nearby trees swayed in the gentle breeze. Nothing else moved. It was dark all around her, but she could just make out a horse and cart. She breathed a sigh of relief.

Suddenly a sack was rammed over the top of her. The world went completely black, and her stomach leaped into her mouth. She kicked out as hard as she could, but a strong pair of hands held her tightly, preventing her from moving. She tried to scream but her voice was muffled by the cloth.

'Cover 'er mouth,' growled a man's voice. 'So she can't scream.'

'She's wriggling,' replied another man's voice. 'And she's really little. She keeps slipping!'

'Gag her then!'

'And how exactly d'you want me to do that eh, genius? Can't you see she's got a bag over her head?'

'Well, take it off then!'

'Why did we put it on 'er in the first place then?'

'Well, so we could, we could . . . Shut up and stop asking such daft questions, and just do as I tell you.'

'You always do everything back to front. Put the bag on her head. Now take it off again. Great wizards! Work it out for yourself first!'

'Are you going to argue with everything I say?'

'Yeah, yeah, whatever. But next time it'll be *me* with a plan. And you won't be able to shut me up then.'

'You *never* have a plan.'

'Well, just don't go telling me to shut up, all right? It really annoys me.'

They pulled the bag off her head, and Martina saw the faces of Aton and Svarko looming over her. They looked revolting and smelled even worse. Martina tried to scream – not to seek help, but rather out of disgust. Svarko, the blonde guy with the 'real grit' tattoo, leaned towards her and started to tie a grubby piece of fabric round her face to gag her mouth, while Aton, the bearded, big-eared one, pushed her into the sack, this time feet first.

Martina clawed at them, kicked her legs and tried to headbutt them, but it was an unfair fight. Aton laid her roughly down on the ground and pulled the bag up to her waist as Svarko tried to finish tying the gag as she thrashed around. At one point, Martina managed to grab Aton's beard and she pulled with all her might.

'Her hands,' yelled Aton. 'Grab her hands!'

'I can't!' answered Svarko. 'She's a real wild one!'

'Great wizards!'

'I told you not to wear braids; they're too tempting to pull!'

Aton roared and held her arms tightly, which meant Svarko could easily finish his job. Martina felt the rough, filthy fabric of the gag on her tongue, and felt sick. She whimpered quietly, quieter than the rustling of the leaves. Aton and Svarko looked at her. They bent down and each took an arm, avoiding her kicking legs. No more than a few seconds had passed.

'Should we tie up her legs as well?' asked Svarko. 'This creature's dangerous.'

'Good evening.'

Martina looked up. *That voice* . . . she thought. *I recognize that voice* . . .

Aton and Svarko dropped Martina and, with her legs all tangled up in the bag, she fell on to her bottom on the hard earth.

'Sorry to disturb you, gentlemen, but what's going on here?' The voice spoke again.

'Nothing for you to worry about, big man,' said Svarko. 'Stay out of it.'

It was the fat man with the pale skin who had until very recently been eating his dinner quietly in The Crazy Skull. He laughed into the darkness.

'Walk on by!' Svarko went over to the man. Then, when he remained where he was, Svarko added, 'You don't get it, do you?'

Svarko aimed a blow at the man, but he ducked with a smooth twist of his waist and responded with a punch to Svarko's jaw, leaving a surprised Svarko flat on his back on the ground.

Aton forgot all about Martina and threw himself at the mysterious newcomer, who was waiting calmly for him. The man took hold of Aton's arms and, using the momentum from Aton's run-up, dashed him against the wall. Aton, his earrings hanging from his notorious ears, bounced off the surface and fell to the ground on top of Svarko.

'Get off me, you fool!' said Aton.

'I'm trying, I'm trying . . .' whined Svarko.

Aton stood up again and launched himself at the big man. The two figures began hand-to-hand combat. Martina started to wriggle out of the sack, but a scream of horror from Aton froze the blood in her veins.

'What is it?' asked Svarko.

'His face is coming off!' said Aton.

'What do you mean, coming off?' exclaimed Svarko.

The big man pushed Aton away, and he was left holding a white face between his hands. A face and a bald head.

Martina stifled a scream and kicked at the bag in desperation until she was free of it.

'His skin has come off! Great wizards! It's a monster!' cried Aton.

Aton chucked aside the empty eyes and the toothless mouth, then grabbed hold of his long knife. Svarko copied him, and they both stared at their enemy.

'What? He has another face underneath! He has two faces!' cried Aton.

'That one's called a mask, you idiot,' responded the big man.

Aton looked at the limp white skin now lying on the dry ground. Martina tried to stand up. She would have succeeded in that simple deed, but in that instant the formerly masked man took advantage of the moment to knock Aton off his feet again, who, as he fell, brought Martina down like a pin in a bowling alley.

Martina tried to disentangle herself from Aton while the unknown man undid the buttons on his tunic and, with a swoosh, he shrugged it off completely.

A rounded metallic structure was resting across his shoulders, disguising a slender, athletic body beneath. The 'big man' threw off the rest of his disguise and stood there, his arms open wide.

What? Martina asked herself. The whole situation was making her head spin. When she was finally on her feet again, her back was against the wall and the others were blocking her path. Aton had stood up really quickly. Neither of the two traders were looking at her and perhaps that gave her a narrow chance to escape, but she didn't have much space and either another fighter would knock her down again or one of the blades would get in her way – and that was something Martina really wanted to avoid. Those knives looked threatening and she couldn't really get out of there without risking injury.

And something else stopped her. It wasn't just the fight

and the fact she was pretty much cornered. What truly held her back was that voice. Where had she heard it before? In her panic to get free, she hadn't heard it very clearly. Her mind raced. She had to leave – or try to – no doubt about that, but she also wanted to see who was helping her. Who was this mysterious fool . . .

'It's just a boy . . .' said Aton.

Svarko wrinkled his nose like an angry dog. 'Get 'im!' he yelled.

But before they could reach him the mysterious figure had raised both his arms and pulled out a pair of long swords with curved silver blades that were concealed beneath the metallic structure. Aton and Svarko stopped dead.

'You were saying . . .?' said the figure.

Without waiting for a response he stormed towards the crooks. He twirled the swords, slicing the air before him. His skill was such that Aton and Svarko kept shuffling backwards until the points of the blades came to a halt right in front of their noses. Their short knives now seemed as useful as spoons.

Svarko swallowed.

Martina thought it was, at last, a good time to silently slip away but, then again, it was clear that somebody was trying to help her. Shouldn't she stay close to him, then? What was she going to do, really, running around on her own in the forest in the middle of the night?

'That's a good trick, eh?' said Aton, interrupting her thoughts. 'Very good. Where d'you learn to do that?'

'Here and there, you know how it is,' the mysterious figure replied.

'Did it take you long to learn?'

'A while, yes,' replied the figure.

'Congratulations,' said Aton.

'Why don't you just buy him a drink while you're at it?' snapped Svarko. 'We're trying to have a fight here . . .'

'But that move was just so glori–'

'You're so stupid,' said Svarko. 'For Wizards' sake, you're such an idiot.'

'Don't call me an idiot.'

'Idiot,' repeated Svarko.

'What did you just call me?!'

'Guys, guys,' the swordsman said, trying to calm them down.

'Idiot,' said Svarko again.

'Idiot, eh? Well, take this.' And with that, Aton dropped his knife and landed a punch on Svarko's jaw. Svarko also let go of his blade and the two men began rolling around having a bare-knuckle fight.

'Fellas, fellas, come on . . .' the newcomer tried again.

The fight continued.

'I said, *enough*!'

With the tip of each sword rested against their throats, Aton and Svarko didn't move a muscle.

And neither did Martina. She was still backed up against one wall, watching. She was mesmerized by everything that was going on – it's not every day you get to see a real swordfight – and also horrified, but her eyes were glued to the action.

She couldn't just stay there. She had to do something. Yes, but what?

Svarko raised his hands. 'Please, sir, don't kill us.'

'We're just men, led astray by poor company,' added Aton.

'We'll never cross your path again, sir. We swear it,' pleaded Svarko.

'I don't doubt it,' came the voice threateningly. 'Because if I ever see you again, I won't be as friendly as I'm being now.'

This is friendly? thought Martina.

The figure lowered his swords, and the crooks began to breathe again.

'Now scram, before I regret it.'

Aton and Svarko began to run.

Martina watched them leave and took a deep breath. She then tried to tidy her clothes, brushing off blades of grass.

'I thought they were traders,' she explained. 'Who were transporting goods.'

'Well, yeah,' said the shadow with the swords, as he picked up the discarded knives. 'The goods they transport are human. They're slave traders.'

'Slaves?'

'Yes. Bernarda sold you like livestock.'

Suddenly Martina caught sight of the stranger's face and her eyes goggled. He wasn't that much of a stranger, after all.

'Matías?!' she exclaimed.

'Yeah, surprise, surprise . . .' he said like a clown, putting his weapons away. 'Now, let's get going. Zavro's waiting for us, and we won't reach Kelytong until dawn.'

Eleven
Kelytong

Martina looked at Matías incredulously. The world was spinning a bit too fast now. It was weird enough that *she* was there. She was dealing with it, though. More or less. But *Matías* as well? Just like that? It was plain insane.

'You? You here?' she said.

Matías didn't reply. He was checking to make sure there was nobody around after the fray.

'Hello? What is this? A prank show? How did you get here?' insisted Martina.

'Same as you. I have a portal at home.'

'What? What are you talking about?'

'It's all part of the Prophecy.

'What *prophecy*?' she asked, her voice getting louder.

'Martina, we've got to go. It's not good for us to be hanging around these places at night.'

'What are you doing here? Do you know Novrogod? Are you . . . *from here*?' Martina asked, aware that it sounded crazy, but she no longer cared. 'Answer me, or you'll die right here, right now. I don't care how many swords you have.'

'In case you hadn't noticed, I'm here to rescue you,' stated Matías.

'You? Rescue *me*?' said Martina in astonishment.

'Yes. I have to protect you so you can carry out your mission,' said Matías in a matter-of-fact voice.

'Mission? What mission?'

'Well, when we ge–'

'I can look after myself,' interrupted Martina.

'Yeah, yeah. Course you can. Can we go now?' asked Matías.

'Ha! You're in charge of protecting me and I almost end up in the hands of some slave traders? Some protection!' snorted Martina.

Matías licked his upper lip.

'This is a secret mission . . .'

'Secret mission, what secret mission?' snapped Martina.

'Well, like the name suggests: it's of the *secret* kind.'

'Yes, yes, everything is so secretive. Mission, prophecy, portal, wizardry, what's next? A spaceship?'

'I understand you are a bit upset –'

'Upset!'

'But, trust me, you'll get your questions answered in good time. Now, we need to move. It's better for Bernarda to believe you're now a slave. Aton and Svarko will never admit they lost you in a fight against just me.'

'I don't see how it's going to be a secret mission if

Bernarda already knows we're heading to Kelytong. I told her that myself.'

'Bernarda has no idea what Kelytong is, or where it is. She took a stab in the dark. Nobody knows. Now, Martina, we really do have to get moving.'

'How did you know I'd be here at The Crazy Skull?'

'I just knew,' replied Matías simply.

For a while, they trudged along the path running parallel to the River of Dark Waters, following its course as the clouds cleared in the sky.

'But how did you know I wouldn't go upstream? Or in any other direction?' Martina asked eventually.

'You were supposed to be The Sent One. That was the direction you had to take,' Matías replied.

'What if I'd taken another route though?'

'Then you wouldn't be my responsibility.'

'Thanks. I feel so much more *protected* now.'

They walked another half an hour in silence. The forest was so thick that to Martina's eyes it seemed impassable. Despite the gurgling of the river, it was impossible to see the water. They heard animals, but Martina chose to ignore them.

'I didn't know you could handle a sword so well.'

'I've been training a long time for this day.'

'While I haven't done any training at all.'

'You're always so negat–'

'Has it occurred to you that I might not want anything to do with all this, but here I am all the same?'

'Well, well, what a temper. You'll get some training,

don't you worry about that. You see, the thing is, until you appeared, nobody knew who The Sent One was. They just knew you'd be someone close to me because I'd been chosen to protect you.'

'So I'm close to you now?'

'Well, our lives did become closer over the last couple of months, yes. It's all part of the Prophecy.'

'So my parents splitting up – that was a prophecy?'

'Well, there's no way to really know, I'll give you that, but we were going to meet, somehow – that much I'm pretty sure of. The two cubes, yours and mine, they contain Wizardry and are like magnets, attracting one another. As I said, it's a prophecy.'

'You say that like it's science! But what if I'm *not* The Sent One?'

'When I saw you, in my house, I mean, I felt sure it was you.'

Martina thought back to the times Matías had spoken to her when she'd visited her dad every weekend. Even the time he'd congratulated her on defending herself well. In all those months, how many words had he spoken to her? Not many. Close to none.

'Does your family know about this? Does Nicole know?' Martina asked.

'Of course not. I am the only one who comes here. I got my cube from my grandad, who was Novrogodian and gave it to me as a present.'

Martina sighed. She was feeling wearier and wearier.

'I still don't understand what this place is.'

'You'll see.'

'What do I need to know about Novrogod?'

'That appearances can be deceiving. You saw what happened in The Crazy Skull. Right, we're here. That over there is Kelytong.'

Martina followed Matías's gaze over to the opposite side of the river. In the warm light of dawn, all Martina could make out was the vegetation covering both sides of the path.

'Over where?'

'Martina, Martina . . . Appearances can be deceiving.'

She remained silent as Matías entered the thicket. Martina followed him, albeit rather reluctantly. They walked for a good while through the greenery, Matías in the lead, slicing his way through the undergrowth with his blades. A few timid rays of sunlight began to warm their backs and Martina got the distinct impression they were walking around in circles.

'Seriously? Do you even know where you're going?' she asked Matías after a bit.

Just then, the woodland ended abruptly. Before her eyes, an enormous clearing opened up. To one side was a lake, a stable and a hut not dissimilar to the others Martina had seen in the village. She took a few steps forward. The green grass grazed her ankles, the sun glinted on the still surface of the lake and smoke curled upward from the chimney.

'Welcome to Kelytong,' said Matías with a smile.

Without waiting for a response, he headed towards the hut. A man came striding out – a man whom Martina recognized . . . from her dream. Could it be the same man who had talked about the Mark of Light? Matías greeted him with a hug. Then the man turned to Martina with a cautious smile.

'It's good that you're here. My name is Zavro.'

Martina was still feeling grumpy, but the place helped to soothe her.

'Hi,' she said.

'She's a bit –' started Matías.

'A bit what?' jumped in Martina.

Matías touched his temple a couple of times.

'Chipi chipi.'

'I'm not *chipi chipi*. What does *chipi chipi* even mean?'

'Martina,' answered Zavro. 'You are The Sent One. This was always going to be difficult, bu–'

'I'm getting a bit fed up with everyone calling me that. My name is Martina.'

Zavro crossed his arms and looked at Matías. 'Was she like this on the way here?' he asked.

Matías nodded seriously and replied, 'The whole way.'

'Yes, before I was basically kidnapped by slave traders . . .'

'That, as I've been trying to explain –' began Matías.

'So excuse me if I wasn't exactly Winnie the Pooh,' interrupted Martina.

'You can say that again . . .'

'I wasn't exactly Winnie the Pooh. There. I said it. Happy now?'

'Do I look happy? Take a wild guess.'

Martina grunted and looked at Zavro, openly ignoring Matías.

'So, what exactly are we doing here?' she asked.

'All in good time,' replied Zavro. 'You must be exhausted.'

She nodded; he was right. Zavro sweetened his expression. His silvery beard, long and well-groomed, lent him a curiously joyful air.

'And hungry?'

Martina remembered the biscuits in her bag.

'I made breakfast,' Zavro said, and smiled.

Twelve
The mission

After a delicious breakfast, Martina went for a lie-down in a bedroom that had been specially prepared for her. There was a bed with a woollen mattress and clean sheets. She also found a pile of clothing waiting for her, the sort they wore in Novrogod: trousers made from a coarse cloth, an embroidered shirt, a black poncho, socks and leather boots.

It was difficult to know what to really think about anything; her mind seemed to explode with ideas and questions. Despite this, Martina slept until sunset. When she awoke she felt fresh and recovered and fully aware of where she was. She dismissed all the was-it-a-dream nonsense questions. She was in Novrogod and she embraced it. Sometimes people have to accept things as they come and Martina was certain she was where she was meant to be. If someone had offered to take her back home, to her surprise, she realized, she would've refused. She was eager to understand what was going on. There was a lot to discover – although she didn't know precisely what awaited her. One thing was clear: puzzling over things was not going to magically sort anything out. She would have to, well, figure out what to do as she went along. Despite having felt a bit grumpy about the way things had been up to that point, now a sense of adventure enveloped her.

She dressed and came out into the warm light and crisp air. She filled her lungs and spotted Matías fishing in the lagoon. For a second she felt disoriented and homesick. She wondered if her mum would be worried, but then she remembered her last visit to Novrogod had lasted for hours and yet, back at home, only two minutes had passed.

Zavro walked over to her, smiling.

'How did you sleep?' he asked her.

'All right,' she replied.

'Excellent. Well, I guess your head is filled with questions. You'll have some answers soon. But first, let's eat.'

Martina nodded, pleased to be able to distract her mind. There was fish with capers, coleslaw, sweetcorn and boiled potatoes. There was also water and freshly baked bread. For dessert, they devoured an apple tart. The sun had already disappeared from the sky as they finished their meal.

Martina sighed, feeling full, and went to sit by the fire with the others. The fire had almost died out, but it wasn't very cold. In fact, the temperature was really rather pleasant. Matías, who had stopped fishing and joined them for dinner, was now chewing on a stick.

'I imagine you have hundreds of questions,' said Zavro.

'How do you clean your teeth here? I know it's a silly one to start, but I'd really like to know.'

'With one of these,' Matías replied, and showed her the stick he was chewing. 'It's called kerpa. It's a bit like a plant they have in Africa. First of all you remove the bark and then you make a couple of notches at one end. The point ends up looking like a toothbrush and can be used to clean your teeth. The sap inside it contains an antiseptic. It works better than toothpaste.'

'Any more questions?' asked Zavro.

'Are you from Novrogod?' Martina asked Matías.

'No,' he replied.

'How did you get here?' Martina asked.

'I told you – the same way you did: through the portal,' said Matías.

'Through the cube and the River of Dark Waters?'

'Exactly,' said Matías.

'How did you get a cube?' asked Martina.

'As I told you, my grandfather was a warrior from Novrogod. Nobody knew except me,' replied Matías.

'I still don't understand anything,' grumbled Martina.

'I think you probably need a full explanation,' said Zavro.

'Yes,' agreed Martina. 'I think I do.'

Matías sighed. Zavro smiled briefly and then shrugged.

Matías started speaking. 'OK, so, I think the story starts with the Brotherhood.'

'I don't know what the Brotherhood is,' Martina said. She tried to keep her voice as innocent and sweet as possible, though it was frustrating to have been left out of, apparently, so much information for so long. She was determined to fix that, though.

'That's what I'm about to tell you,' said Matías in exasperation.

'Oh.'

Matías looked at her like she were trying to wind him up on purpose. If that was her intention, it seemed to be working.

'If I may continue. The Brotherhood was formed by a group of Wizards who were experimenting with Wizardry.'

'Er, um . . .' broke in Martina.

'What?'

'I don't know what Wizardry is.'

Zavro suppressed a smile as he saw the look on Matías's face.

'Wizardry is a type of energy that exists in Novrogod for the good of all Novrogodians,' replied Matías. 'It can cure illnesses, bring rain to water crops, that sort of thing. Basically, it connects those who live in Novrogod with nature. D'you get it?'

'Yes, thank you. You can go on now.'

Matías sighed. 'Great, so, the only people who can handle this energy are Wizards because it takes a long time to learn how to use it. A particular group of Wizards – the Experimenters – had moved beyond merely controlling Wizardry. They were studying it, experimenting, searching for new possibilities. They became known as the Brotherhood. Their main task was to help Novrogod and to teach the ordinary Wizards new tricks, if you like.'

'How many Experimenters were there in the Brotherhood?' Martina asked.

'Six. It was a very select group. The thing is, though, the Brotherhood started to close in on itself and began to use Wizardry purely for its own benefit and not for the greater good. They didn't want to share their power. I guess they started to think, why bother? The Experimenters were the best at handling Wizardry, so why worry about everyone else? Why answer to anybody else?

'Socrates was the first and only Experimenter who split off from the Brotherhood when he saw it closing ranks – they were forgetting the very reason for its existence. He even went as far as to confront his former colleagues, which led to him defeating them at the Battle of Black Rock.'

'How did he manage that?' asked Martina. 'Surely the Brotherhood had the upper hand, what with their knowledge of Wizardry. And wouldn't that make it five against one?'

'Well, really, it was more like six against one.'

'But didn't you just say there were six Experimenters in the Brotherhood, not seven?'

'There was one Wizard who was training to enter the Brotherhood. It was just as that Wizard began to spend time with the Experimenters that the Brotherhood closed ranks. Nobody ever knew their name. They were simply known as the seventh Wizard.'

'Well, that works in my favour. So, there was a battle, six-to-one . . .'

'Exactly, but don't forget, Socrates was an Experimenter too. In fact, he was the best. And he had the support of all the other Wizards in Novrogod, the non-Experimental ones. It wasn't easy but together they defeated the Brotherhood.'

'What happened to the Experimenters?'

'They died,' said Matías simply. 'All except one.'

'The seventh Wizard.'

'Yes. That same one whose name nobody knew because he'd never told anyone. His colleagues had even made up a name for him: Voraz.'

Matías sighed again, then continued. 'After the Brotherhood had been defeated, he was never seen again. Socrates had never been entirely satisfied with that explanation, though. He just didn't trust Voraz. He insisted that one rogue Experimenter alone – even just a trainee – could be more dangerous than the entire Brotherhood put together because it was easier to stay hidden. So Socrates decided to take certain precautions, just in case Voraz ever reappeared. He worked until he achieved his purpose, storing Wizardry in a butterfly that was inaccessible to the Wizards. He called it the Butterfly of Light.

'According to the Prophecy, the Wizardry stored in the Butterfly of Light will set aflame the Sword of Fire, which will burn – even under water – and reduce everything it touches to ash. The Sword of Fire will defeat Voraz. However, the Butterfly of Light will only awaken with the arrival of The Sent One, who will supposedly arrive in Novrogod if Voraz ever returns. So, Socrates sent two Novrogodians far, far away, to a place where Voraz could never find them.'

'To another world.'

'You're starting to get it, yes. A Wizard and a warrior. He sent them each without knowing the location of the other, but close enough for their paths to cross. He gave each one a cube and a mirror. My grandfather was the warrior, and that's how I got my cube.'

'So that means my Grandma Famke was . . .' said Martina thoughtfully.

'The Wizard, yes.'

'Don't be ridiculous. She can't have been. She was European.'

'But from where, exactly?'

'Well, her village disappeared in the war, and –'

'What a coincidence,' Matías interrupted.

Martina rubbed her hand across her forehead. So many new ideas were making her head spin. She wasn't really hungry – quite the opposite, actually – but she started stuffing cold leftovers into her mouth. It didn't really matter what, she just had to eat something.

'I think we need to take it a bit easier,' said Zavro.

Martina turned towards him.

'How do you know all of this – the Prophecy?' she asked.

'In the same way as all prophecies are known, Martina,' said Zavro, smiling. 'Some people sang it, over and over, everywhere. Some people listened and told it to little children. Stories live, Martina, because people share them.'

'How did Matías know he was supposed to be here?' Martina asked.

'Simple. One day I was playing with the cube –' said Matías.

'Cubes have Wizardry in them, Martina,' intervened Zavro. 'They recognize the right people. And they help connect them through dreams, as well.'

Martina exhaled, then said, 'Where are we? Kelytong, I mean. Why did I have to come here?'

'My dear Martina,' replied Zavro. 'This is a training camp. You have come here so you can awaken the Butterfly of Light and, in doing so, set aflame the Sword of Fire.'

'What's the Sword of Fire? I mean, a sword cannot be *made* of fire.'

'Nobody knows,' answered Matías.

'What do you mean, *nobody knows*?' Martina asked.

'Only Socrates knew,' replied Matías calmly. 'And now he's dead. Not even Princess Emelia knows and she's heir to the throne of Novrogod.'

'So what are we going to do?'

'Follow the Prophecy,' said Zavro. 'Socrates left behind the Butterfly of Light, under guard at the Mountain of Destiny. It's been there for years, waiting for The Sent One to arrive. And when this butterfly is released, it will give you the power to set aflame the Sword of Fire. And then you will be invincible.'

'But until then, as you can see, sweet cheeks, we've got more than enough work to do and very little time,' added Matías.

'Don't call me sweet cheeks.'

'Whatever. Look, nobody knows exactly what the Sword of Fire looks like because nobody has ever seen it. Everyone who has ever tried to get to the Butterfly has died – kaput, ciao, see you later. But we do know the location of the Mountain of Destiny. And that's where you come in, Martina.'

'You are The Sent One,' concluded Zavro. 'You have the Mark of Light. You emerged from the River of Dark Waters during the night of the crescent moon. And now, you are here.'

'What would have happened if I had never come here?' Martina asked.

'The only answer I can give you is that you came,' replied Zavro.

'My mission was to watch you as soon as I suspected you were The Sent One,' added Matías.

'Well, thanks a lot for all your help. I don't know if I'd have managed without you,' Martina snorted sarcastically.

'I can only help you in extreme situations,' said Matías.

'Only? Aren't you my protector, blah, blah, blah?'

'Here, yes, but not in Montevideo.'

'Why not? Is it out of your so-called jurisdiction? You're Batman and never work outside Gotham City?' asked Martina.

'If I had helped you, the Prophecy wouldn't have come true. It's a Prophecy, don't you see? It has to find its own way. Imagine if I helped you and you ended up not being The Sent One? What then?'

'That's precisely my concern.'

'Well, since you're here now, I guess we'll finally find out, won't we?'

'OK, what were these *extreme situations*, then? When exactly *could* you help me out?' demanded Martina.

'You're right. I couldn't really do anything. In Montevideo, I mean.'

'Not even if I died?'

'Were you in danger of dying?'

'I don't know. Was I?'

'Guys, guys, arguing won't get us anywhere . . .' said Zavro.

'I get it,' said Martina. 'I have to go and look for this old Butterfly of Light over at the Mountain of Destiny, light up the Sword of Fire and save Novrogod. Is that right? Ooh, I do hope there'll be a dragon to slay, or I might just die of boredom on the way.'

'The tugs will be looking for us,' said Matías. 'And there'll be plenty of problems on the way, don't you worry.'

'Great. So, when do we go?' asked Martina.

'Not yet,' replied Matías. 'First you have to train.'

'Train?' repeated Matina warily.

Matías smiled, then replied, 'Tomorrow. And I'm the trainer.'

Thirteen
Training

That night Martina slept like a log. After a generous breakfast – which seemed the norm here in Kelytong – she prepared herself for the first day of training. For some incomprehensible reason, Matías seemed to be looking forward to it.

'Right then, are you ready?' he asked her.

'What exactly do I have to do?' she replied.

'First off: listen.'

'I'm listening.'

'With a positive attitude.'

'I have a positive attitude.'

'Hmm . . . We'll see about that,' he said. He cleared his throat. 'There are several different areas of training. Zavro will be in charge of the mental part, and I'll be in charge of your physical skills.'

'So, I'm not completely under your control then.'

'Well, no –'

'Because yesterday it sounded like I was going to have to bow to you before speaking to you, you know, like *The Karate Kid* or something.'

'You see? This is listening with a negative attitude. You're being combative.'

'Ooh, my apologies, Master Jedi,' Martina said, bowing.

Matías huffed and looked towards Zavro, who was watching the start of Martina's training.

Zavro smiled serenely, then said, 'It seems to me that you two need to be alone and calm, don't you think?'

Martina folded her arms and looked at Matías.

'So, what exactly do I need to do, Master Trainer?'

'What you have to learn took me years to learn – that is, considering the time I've been here and training at home –'

Martina put her hands on her hips and said, 'Can you train at home?'

'I don't work with Wizardry, so, yes, I can. I did. I trained in Montevideo. A lot. I came here, to Novrogod, basically to understand what was going on and . . . and, really, I don't think we have time for personal histories here, we only have a few days, so if you don't help me –'

'Aha, so you need my help. Did I hear anyone say please?' Martina said.

Matías glared at her and said in a monotone, 'There are different areas of training. We aren't going to look at all of them. What is particularly important right now is speed. If you can move quickly, you'll be in a position to win.'

Matías walked over to a leather bag he'd brought with him. He took out some different-coloured balls, about the same size as snooker balls. There were five in total. He placed three in his right hand and two in his left and looked over at Martina, who was still standing with her hands on her hips.

Matías then threw one of the balls from his left hand up into the air. Soon all five balls were suspended, forming a perfect arc, hanging there as if by magic. He held them in mid-air for a few seconds, his face betraying no hint of effort, then collected all five balls in his hands as before and handed three to Martina.

'We'll try with just these three to start with,' he said.

'What? Am I some sort of circus performer now?'

'It's called general training. Now. Three. That's all.'

If he could do it with five, it couldn't be that hard, surely.

Martina took the balls confidently. They weren't particularly heavy or hard. She threw them up into the air and tried to do what Matías had done with apparent ease. The balls bounced off her head and on to the ground. Her face flushed and she quickly gathered them up. Matías had sat down and was staring out across the lake.

'Try again,' he said.

After several minutes, during which the balls kept falling, almost always right on to her head, Matías allowed her to start with just two balls and showed her how to hold her hands. He also told her how to place her feet, so she was firmly supported, and instructed her to look up, not down. With two balls, Matías's instructions and some patience, Martina managed to do something very similar to what Matías had done before.

She may only be using two balls, but a sense of triumph overcame her. She looked at Matías, expecting some sort of recognition or acknowledgement of her talents, but all he did was look at her with a touch of boredom in his eyes and nod.

'I would, now and then, welcome a little motivation, you know?' said Martina.

Matías looked at her without much expression.

'Better get better, or you might die out in the wild. How's that for a pep talk?' he replied.

A surge of anger drowned Martina's sense of triumph. However, this time, she focused on trying even harder. She'd show him in the end. Then he'd see.

This went on and on, day after day. The time passed slowly, and Martina ended up feeling like she was at school. She had to train all day long while Zavro watched smilingly over their sessions from a distance.

Dear Diary,

Well, the whole 'Dear Diary' thing is really just a saying, because my actual diary is back at home (I always forget something when I go away). But anyway, I managed to find this paper and a sort of pencil so that I can keep doing one thing I do at home, which helps me not miss it so much.

So here I am. I'm doing nothing but training.

Matías never seems to get tired, but I am exhausted (thanks for everything). When night falls it's like I plunge into a coma, and when it's time to get up it's like I only went to sleep fifteen minutes ago.

Some of the exercises are really weird. For example, there's one where I have to go into the lake so the water is up to my waist and wait for the grey fish to come close to me – they're the ones that leap out from the surface of the water. They're super-fast and the exercise is all about me trying to touch one. Matías doesn't just touch them, he grabs hold of them too – he makes it look so easy – and then lets them go back into the water. And that's not all: I'm fed up with the whole issue of there not being any decent bathrooms. Washing in the river is not really that much fun, to tell you the truth. No hot water or showers. Not to mention shampoo.

Right, well here comes the 'trainer' again. But I am getting better, little by little. I can do three balls at a time now – yay.

Another of Matías's ideas was to climb a five-metre-tall pole with straw spread out underneath it in case she fell. Much to Martina's disgust, they repeated the exercise several times a day.

'What's this exercise even for?' she asked furiously. 'It's completely pointless.'

'No, it's not,' replied Matías.

'Didn't you say we had to train in speed?'

'How exactly do you think you're going to climb the Mountain of Destiny? In a lift?'

One night after dinner, when they were sitting quietly, Martina asked Matías, 'What happens if I'm not The Sent One? Do you ever think of that?'

'Martina, you wouldn't be here if you weren't.'

'Ugh, you're so sure of it all.'

'I believe in the Prophecy. You're here; that's proof enough to me.'

'Always so scientific.'

'Scientists believe what they can see. I see you here. That's proof enough to me.'

Martina didn't answer immediately. She had to admit to herself that he had a point. Matías softened and looked at her.

'Also . . . you'll surprise yourself, I think. It's all a matter of focus. You're doing really well.'

This is what she was thinking about the next morning as she tried to touch the fish in the lake. By this point she just got on with it without thinking too much.

'It's all just a matter of focus, Martina,' Matías said from a distance. 'You have to concentrate, Martina. Concentrate.'

Martina took a deep breath and closed her eyes. *Concentrate*. Of course, like it's that easy. She breathed slowly. The sounds around her faded away, almost into nothingness. Martina forgot about her wet clothes making her feel uncomfortable. She opened her eyes and fixed her gaze on a certain point in the water. She inhaled slowly, allowing the air to fill her lungs and flood her with energy. She focused on the surface of the lake. Everything around her had turned fuzzy. She saw a fish leap out of the water and stretched out her right hand, certain she was going to miss it.

But she didn't. She felt the cold scales on her hand, pushed it through the air and, suddenly, the fish was flying as if it had been shot out of a catapult. Martina stood still for a moment and watched the fish plop back into the lake with a splash. She turned to a smiling Matías.

For the first time since she had arrived in Novrogod, she ate supper feeling truly happy.

'The first thing you need to know when you're fighting with a sword is how to stand properly,' said Matías, who was in front of her.

They had just started fencing. Matías had given her a wooden blade and they had fought several times, always with the same results: Martina's sword would go flying through the air and land on the ground a few metres away. Faced with the evidence of her previous exercises, rather than protest, she gave in and decided to try and learn from Matías. If she didn't, they'd spend the whole day like this.

'Go on then, how do I do it?' Martina asked.

'Don't stand straight on; stand sideways,' he replied.

Matías moved her shoulders to show her how, and Martina took a deep breath. She'd never been this close to him before. Then, silently, he stepped away and looked at her before continuing, 'Now it'll be easier for you to protect yourself with the sword. Lunge it forward and that's it. Your attacker won't be able to reach your chest or your stomach. By stretching out your arm you'll force them to keep their distance. You see?'

It worked.

'But you still have a problem,' he said.

'What's that?'

Matías placed his hand on her right shoulder and gave her a gentle shove, almost making her fall.

'What are you doing?'

'Your feet aren't in the right position. They're in a straight line, which is why it's so easy to unbalance you. Put your front foot pointing forward, and your back one facing out. Like this.'

Matías demonstrated and she copied. When he pushed her this time, she managed to keep her balance without any problem. Next Matías explained how to lunge forward, bending her front knee to attack and bending the back leg to retract. Martina was fighting much more efficiently now.

'Very good, Martina. Very good,' said Matías.

'Really?'

'Mm-hmm. I think you'll be ready soon. Or maybe you won't. Either way, we have to get moving.'

Martina was in her room preparing her things for the journey when Zavro came in. He watched her for a few moments before saying, 'I heard you ask Matías the other day about what would happen if you were not The Sent One.'

'How did you hear that? Matías and I were alone.'

'I hear a lot of things, but that is not the point. You doubt yourself.'

Martina shrugged. 'Maybe.'

'Do you know what makes a hero stand out from everyone else?'

Martina looked at him thoughtfully. She remembered the heroes from comics. She hadn't read them much; she didn't really like them.

'I don't know.'

'Think about it.'

Martina sighed and took a moment to think.

'They can do things that other people can't,' she said.

'But villains can also do things that other people can't.'

'I don't know then.'

'Heroes sacrifice themselves for the good of everyone else. They help other people. Why are you here, Martina? Why did you come?'

'Because . . .'

'Because Emelia needed help. Am I right? I bet she told you they were expecting you, that you are The Sent One and who knows what else. Didn't she? I bet she did. And she was perfectly honest with you. That's why you know you have a role to play in all this, Martina. If you want to, of course. Because it's not without its risks. It would've been understandable if you had decided to walk out. It would be fine if you ignored this altogether and left right now. However, you are here. You came. You stayed. You are persisting. You see? What matters is not what you say or think, but what you do. Your actions – you, in the end – are the very answer to your own doubts.'

Fourteen
The journey begins

They left on horseback. Martina's horse was white with brown patches, while Matías rode a horse the colour of wet sand. They were carrying food and warm clothes in saddlebags and pockets – Martina left behind her backpack because it would have attracted too much attention – and a sword each.

Dawn was breaking. Zavro stayed at the camp and Martina wondered how it would feel to leave him behind. He was one of the few friends she had in Novrogod. Be that as it may, she was journeying to the Mountain of Destiny with Matías. And once they reached it? Well, they'd see. Nobody had even seen the Butterfly of Light before – they had only ever heard about it.

Matías rode along quietly, his eyes facing forward. They emerged on to the footpath and went in the opposite direction to The Crazy Skull. Martina glanced behind her. She couldn't see anything special, just a tongue of beaten earth winding among the oak and chestnut trees.

Matías fell into his usual silence, which Martina interpreted as annoyance, *incomprehensible* annoyance. Why was he in such a mood? Things seemed to be going well, didn't they? Would they ride the whole way to the Mountain of Destiny in silence? Time passed by more slowly than she had expected, and she soon began to feel bored.

'What's this path called, anyway?' asked Martina eventually.

She realized Matías's eyes were actually sweeping from side to side.

'The Path of Life,' he replied.

'What a strange name!'

'Wasn't me who named it.'

Martina got used to the silence around them and began to distinguish the different sounds of the horses' hooves on the earth, the river to her right and the various animals around her. She didn't know if they were noises to be frightened of or not, but Matías appeared calm.

'In the Wizard Socrates' time, this path was enchanted: whoever walked along it would be protected,' explained Matías. 'No animal would ever attack them. Now only the remains of the enchantment exist. There're no guarantees any more.'

They rode on until nightfall, not even stopping to eat. The sun travelled across the sky from one side to the other. The few times that Martina felt hungry, she took a biscuit from her jacket pocket and ate it on horseback.

When the sun sank into the horizon, they turned towards the River of Dark Waters. They reached the riverbank, let the horses drink and sat down to rest. They had some woven blankets, and after eating some of the cold roasted meats they had brought with them they prepared for the night. Matías lit a small fire, protected from the wind by a stone circle that also served to hide the flames. They settled down round it. Every muscle in Martina's body ached.

'How much more of this until we reach the Mountain of Destiny?' she asked.

'A few days,' Matías replied.

'I didn't know it was so far.'

'It's a long way, but the real problem is that we won't be able to travel every day like we have today.'

'Why not?'

'Because we're just entering the Abandoned Territories. I don't think the enchantment from the Path of Life will cover us that far. This is the wildest part of Novrogod.'

Tied to two trees, the horses seemed fearful and whinnied. Matías broke off from his explanation and glanced away.

'What is it?' asked Martina.

Matías didn't answer. He stood up and placed his hand on the hilt of his sword as he scanned the undergrowth. Martina looked around as well, but all she saw was leaves and branches. And darkness. She stood up and moved next to Matías.

'What is it?' she insisted.

'Shh.'

Matías pointed to one of his own ears. Martina held her breath and turned her head so that one of her ears pointed in the same direction as Matías's.

'I can't hear anyth–'

But just then she heard a sound coming from a mound of logs, branches and bushes immediately in front of her. It was a quiet, rustling sound, like someone or something moving slowly. She swallowed.

'Martina,' said Matías quietly. 'Get behind me.'

He was staring into the foliage. Martina peered again into the thicket. Some of the leaves were quivering, but only some. Then, at one side, a bush shook, and they heard running footsteps. And then, silence.

Martina didn't wait for Matías to say it twice – she slid in behind him.

'What is it?' she asked for the third time, in a whisper.

'There's something there.'

'Really? Well done, Sherlock.'

Matías turned his head slowly to look at her witheringly, and Martina feared he might just be about to use his sword on her instead.

'What? It's obvious there's *something* there,' she said, justifying her question.

Matías blinked incredulously. Then Martina saw two yellow spots gleaming in the darkness.

'There,' she said.

'Where?' replied Matías.

The two yellow spots had disappeared again. Martina

felt Matías's heavy breathing as they both tried to make out the movements in the darkness.

'I *think* it has yellow eyes,' said Martina.

The horses pulled at the reins tying them to the trees, their hooves pawing at the ground.

'I see you,' whispered Matías into the darkness. 'I see you.'

Martina looked behind her. They were right on the edge of the River of Dark Waters. There was no escape; whatever was after them, they were just going to have to face it. She tried to remember everything from her fencing lessons, but she was so nervous she couldn't even remember how to stand.

'That's it,' muttered Matías. 'Come out here where I can see you . . .'

Then, as if with the sole intention of pleasing Matías, the creature appeared in the pale light of the moon. Its head was lowered, its ears pinned back. Its eyes, two gleaming dots, sparkled and its teeth snapped at the air.

'Socrates . . .?' exclaimed Martina.

The eyes flickered briefly towards her before settling back on Matías.

'What did you say?' asked Matías.

'Socrates . . .?' repeated Martina.

He was skinnier than the first time Martina had seen him, but it was without a doubt the same dog that had accompanied her to the River of Dark Waters. Martina took a step forward and the dog looked at her again.

'Martina, you're making me nervous. What are you doing?' asked Matías.

'I know this dog.'

'Martina, no. Don't go any closer.'

But she ignored him. Socrates *must* have recognized her, just as she had recognized him. She walked towards the dog, who was still growling and baring his teeth.

'Socrates . . .? It's me, Martina.'

The dog stared at Martina and stopped growling. Matías shifted his weight and a thunderous rumbling once again filled the animal's throat. His hackles went up and he tensed the muscles in his legs.

'Matías, stay still. You're making him nervous.'

'I'm making *him* nervous?'

'Socrates, it's me. Everything's going to be all right.'

She took a few more steps and the dog crouched down. Martina stopped. *It looks like he's about to pounce and plunge his teeth into my neck,* she thought. She looked the dog straight in the eyes as she wondered whether or not to move forward again.

'Martina . . .' warned Matías.

Again, she ignored him; she was too focused on the dog. She buried her gaze in the creature's yellow eyes and the two remained motionless. Yes, it was definitely Socrates. Martina clenched her jaw and reached out her hand towards him, her fingers bent. She knew that dogs perceive outstretched human fingers as claws and they attack to defend themselves.

Martina continued to move her bent hand towards Socrates' muzzle. If the dog caught her scent, there wouldn't be a problem. He must recognize her. Her hand was no further than a metre from him. Martina reached out a little further, until she was almost touching him. The animal was still crouched in his attack position, but he didn't make a move. There was no other choice than to keep moving her hand forward because pulling back now would have invited the dog to pounce. She advanced a few more centimetres until the dog let out a whine and covered his teeth. Martina smiled, reached out to him and rubbed his neck, at the same time as Socrates licked her hand.

'Socrates, Socrates. Hello there, little doggy –'

'*Doggy?*' asked Matías, stowing his sword. 'That's the biggest dog I've ever seen.'

'Why can't we take him with us?' asked Martina.

It was cloudy and Martina feared it was about to rain for the first time since she had arrived in Novrogod. It would be no fun at all riding all day long in the rain. Her throat hurt, her ears too, and her neck ached from having slept on the hard ground. A meagre breakfast of nothing more than a few dry biscuits and a little hot tea had left her feeling grumpy.

'I already told you,' replied Matías wearily. 'The journey's too long and he'll hold us up.'

He was quiet that morning and he ate his breakfast in a mood, sitting on a log, still wrapped up in his blanket. He clasped his cup of tea and didn't look at her as he spoke.

'I don't see why he'd hold us up,' said Martina.

In the cold morning, the dog's body radiated heat,

resting as he was against her blanket. His breath formed a weak cloud of vapour and she fed him a dry biscuit, which Socrates devoured in a single bite. He seemed happy.

'I don't think he'll hold us up,' she insisted.

'Oh yes, he will.'

'Ugh. What if you're wrong? Haven't you ever been wrong before?'

'What if we have to make a quick exit on horseback? Can he run as fast as a horse? Can he keep walking all day? What happens if he gets distracted by a bird or something and makes us go more slowly? And what if he gets hurt? What are you going to do then, eh? Take him to a vet?'

Martina swallowed her tea and chewed on a biscuit. The dog looked at her, his ears pricked upward.

'He won't hold us up,' said Martina, stroking the dog's head. Socrates wagged his tail. It was so heavy it was almost like a whip. 'Hey Socrates, you beautiful boy.'

'What happens if we have to cross a river? If he drowns, he drowns. Sorry, but he does.'

'He won't drown.'

'If we have to cut through the forest and he gets lost, we're not stopping to look for him.'

'He won't get lost. And anyway, he can protect us.'

Matías sighed.

'His sense of smell is better than ours,' said Martina. 'He can see better in the dark. These animals have additional senses and they can orientate themselves naturally. He's better equipped than us for wild terrain, and there's no good reason for us to go turning down a bit of extra help.'

Matías walked over to the horses, saying, 'I won't feed him from my supplies. And I suggest you don't either.'

'He can feed himself. He's clearly kept himself alive so far.'

Matías looked at the dog, who lifted his cold eyes towards him. After a few seconds of mutual study, a noise emerged from Socrates' throat. It was a warning, not a threat. Matías looked at the dog, unmoved.

'If it bites me, or even tries, it'll be dog stew for supper. Got it?'

Fifteen
The first enemies

As Martina had feared, it did rain in the end. All day long, in fact. It was a fine rain, not too heavy to stop their journey, so they continued onwards in the wet. There was no breeze and the raindrops seemed to fall lazily, as if suspended in the air. As the hours went by, a strong scent of damp earth rose up from the ground.

They didn't speak much. Socrates trotted happily alongside Martina's horse without any problem at all. Around midday the rain grew heavier, and Matías decided – much to Martina's joy – that it didn't make sense to continue. They stopped and built an improvised shelter using some branches and blankets, where they ate their lunch and waited for the rain to ease off.

As the two humans cleaned their teeth with kerpa, Matías said, 'Be careful not to swallow any of it.'

'Why?'

'It's a laxative.'

'What do you mean?'

'If you swallow part of the plant, or if you suck on it, let's just say you'll need a toilet somewhere nearby soon after.'

Just then, Socrates trotted over to Martina. He had a stick between his teeth. They had been playing fetch for a while, Martina throwing the stick and Socrates bringing it back to her. This time he came back and laid the stick between Martina's feet. She patted his head and chucked the stick again. Socrates bounded off after it.

Martina went back to cleaning her teeth with kerpa, carefully.

'Who is Zavro?' she asked, in between rubbing her teeth.

'What do you mean, *who is he*?'

'I mean, where did he come from?'

'He's a Wizard,' Matías said.

'I thought there weren't any Wizards left?'

'Wizards still exist, but they can't do anything if there's no Wizardry for them to work with.'

'So how can Zavro cast spells?'

'He can't do much, and the enchantments he can do aren't very important. Even so, he's a great Wizard who can work with what little Wizardry there is.'

'I had a dream featuring him. Back in Montevideo.'

'The cubes contain stored Wizardry that cannot be stolen but once you activate them, a great Wizard like Zavro could connect through dreams.'

'Why doesn't he come with us then, to help us?'

'Because we can't let Voraz sense any changes to the Wizardry he's using. What Zavro can do is nothing compared to Voraz. He mustn't know we're here until we have the Sword of Fire.'

Socrates returned with the stick and Martina lobbed it, further than she had been doing. The dog hared after it again.

'When did you first meet him?'

'Zavro? The first time I came here. He was waiting for me.'

'How old were you?'

'Six.'

'That's all?'

'When my grandfather died, he left me the cube as a gift. I accidentally activated it and ended up here.'

'And nobody ever explained anything to you?'

'Zavro trained me and explained everything to me.'

'But your parents didn't know anything?'

'No. When my father was born, the Wizard Socrates was still in charge. There had been no need to train him for anything. The same goes for your mum. You mustn't tell anyone else about Novrogod.'

Socrates came back to Martina. This time she didn't throw the stick, instead stroking the dog's fur.

'How long until we reach the Abandoned Territories?'

'We're already there. Nobody comes this far. I've never been here, not even once.'

'I thought you knew the whole place. Aren't you some kind of expert or something?'

'I *am* an expert.'

'How can you be so sure?'

'For the same reason you're so sure of that dog. I just know.'

Later that afternoon it stopped raining and they set off on their journey again. The path was muddy and the horse's hooves sank into the soft, dark earth. The going was slow and took much more effort. Socrates' legs were covered in mud, but he walked on tirelessly next to Martina's horse.

Martina wondered what could possibly go wrong. It seemed a normal, boring journey to her, and she missed having something to read or do, like a crossword. That's what she was thinking about when Matías suddenly pulled to a halt. Martina didn't notice and continued on a few more steps.

'Martina!'

He didn't shout, but he spoke with urgency. Martina instantly pulled on the reins and the horse stopped. She looked over at Matías, whose eyes were glued to the front, before turning to look in the same direction. All she could see was the Path of Life lined with wet earth and forest on both sides.

'What is it?' asked Martina.

'Keep your voice down,' Matías told her, his eyes on the footpath. 'And come over here.'

Martina couldn't tell what was happening. If there even *was* something happening.

'Socrates . . .?'

The dog wasn't there next to her. Alarmed, Martina turned to look back. Socrates had stopped some way back and was standing stock-still, just like Matías, his eyes forward too.

'Socrates . . .?' she urged in a low voice.

No response. Martina tugged twice on the reins and her horse stepped back. She peered into the undergrowth, at the path and even up to the sky, but she couldn't see anything strange . . . other than a dark green-blue mottled blob that leaped from one edge of the path and studied them with its black eyes.

'A frog?' asked Martina. 'You're scared of a *frog*?'

Matías was pale. Martina was going to say something else, but on her other side she heard a familiar sound: a low growling coming from Socrates' throat. His ears were pinned right back flat against his skull.

Martina looked again. It was the biggest frog she'd ever seen. It must have measured at least ten centimetres from the ground to its head, and even more from head to toe. But frogs weren't scary. What was she missing?

'It's a frog . . .' she said, just to make sure her eyes weren't deceiving her.

'Tsk, tsk,' Matías said, shaking his head. 'Wrong.'

He dismounted and took off the poncho he'd been wearing to protect him against the rain and the cold. His hands were now free and he had better access to his sword. Martina copied him.

She still didn't understand what the problem was, though. She looked at the frog again. Its eyes glared back at her. That was the first thing to set alarm bells ringing in Martina's head.

'Do they have . . . teeth?' she asked.

'No. They have fangs.'

'Is that normal?'

'Martina, these are not normal frogs,' said Matías. 'They're zeltogs.'

'Zeltogs?'

'A type of poisonous frog.'

'Very poisonous?'

'Well, I wouldn't recommend letting even one fang graze your skin.'

'Shouldn't we stay on horseback then? It can't get us up there.'

Matías snorted and unsheathed his sword.

'Why are you laughing? And why have you got out your sword?'

'They can kill a horse.'

'Wha–?'

'And they jump high . . . and fast.'

Martina felt a shiver run down her back.

'Well, at least there's only one,' she said.

That was the most inappropriate comment Martina could have made at the most inopportune moment, as several other zeltogs hopped out to join the first, so quickly that Martina lost count before she could get to ten.

'Oh, I forgot to say,' Matías said as he prepared his sword. 'They usually travel in an army.'

Martina looked at the zeltogs.

'Shouldn't we just jump on the horses and turn round?'

'The Mountain of Destiny is that way, though.'

'And there's no other way?'

'No.'

'Can't we turn back and wait for them to go?'

Matías sighed, lowered his sword and turned to face her. 'Martina, they're *hunting* us.'

Martina looked at Matías in surprise. She didn't know exactly how to respond. Matías was not behaving as you'd expect prey to.

'Shouldn't we be more scared, then?'

'Perhaps, yeah.'

'What do you mean, *perhaps, yeah*? Are you enjoying this? Have you gone completely insane?'

Teeth emerged from between Matías's lips, then he said, 'When you come to Novrogod, Martina, you need to embrace the good and the bad.'

Up to this point it hadn't occurred to her that Matías could be nuts, but maybe he was. A little. You probably had to be, if you were coming to another world on a more or less regular basis. Martina swallowed.

'Well, I'm not taking another step. I'm not planning to be an afternoon snack for an army of frogs,' she said.

The first frog hopped towards them, a leap of some two metres, seemingly effortlessly. Matías focused on the frog and stood poised with his sword at the ready. Martina stared at the other frogs.

There must have been more than a hundred now. She

tried to swallow, but her throat had become incredibly tight. Only a thin thread of air could enter.

'What do we do now?' she asked Matías.

'What do you mean, *what do we do*?'

'Well, what's the plan?'

'This.'

Matías turned to her again and held out his right hand. Martina stretched out her own and Matías shook it.

'Good luck!' he said.

And saying nothing more, he turned back to the zeltogs.

'That's it? That's the plan? Saying *good luck*?' Martina exclaimed.

'Didn't you want to find out if you really are The Sent One and if I really am an expert?' Matías said. 'Well, it looks like your wish is coming true.'

The first zeltog jumped again, like it was flying. Three metres now separated it from Matías. It hopped again with so much force that it almost disappeared in flight. Matías drew an arc with his sword, whipping it through the air. It was a quick, precise movement, and the frog was sliced neatly in two. It fell to the ground, its thick, sticky blood mingling with the wet soil.

Martina felt her heart thumping in her chest, but Matías maintained his cool composure, his eyes glued on the zeltogs and his sword ready for more. Her palms sweaty, Martina prepared her sword, but it was hard to grasp the metal in her fist.

The zeltogs were still. Then, without warning, one

suddenly took a couple of violent leaps towards Martina. She saw two perfect rows of teeth like needles searching for her throat. She froze in terror. Her sword felt like lead and her arms felt like they were made of feathers.

She was mentally preparing herself for the sensation of those teeth plunging into her neck when a figure cut in front of her and caught hold of the frog. Martina looked to one side; the frog was dangling from Socrates' jaws. Well, that was two fewer zeltogs, at least. *Perfect, only ninety-eight more.*

'Martina. You see how these things jump towards you?'

'Y-yes.'

'Right, well, when that happens –'

'What?'

'Do something!'

'Oh, right. Was that the plan?'

'It's all a question of focus, Martina. Concentrate.'

The zeltogs glared at them, an icy, black stare. Martina took a deep breath. The sounds around her became muffled and the precise shapes of the forest and frogs blurred. The noise disappeared, leaving Martina unaware of even Socrates or Matías nearby. All she saw was the frogs.

She turned sideways on. Several zeltogs began hopping towards her, but this time Martina was able to anticipate the flow of their jumps, easily following their movements, as if the zeltogs had suddenly begun leaping in slow motion. When the first frog was close enough, she swung her sword and the creature disappeared, sliced in two, its front legs flying off to one side, its back legs to the other.

Martina kept her focus; more were coming. She grasped her sword with both hands and wielded it, rocking her waist from side to side and raising her elbows up and down, making the most of the frogs' momentum as they threw themselves on to her blade.

Martina had no idea how long they had been there or how many fewer zeltogs there now were in Novrogod, but she could see several more, waiting patiently. And then, just as suddenly as the attack had started, it stopped. Martina stood still, waiting for more.

'Martina!'

Somehow she had been able to channel all her energy into the action of fighting, without spending time on thoughts or emotions. At that moment, this achievement sent a pleasant shiver along her back.

'What?'

'Didn't you hear me? I called you three times,' Matías said.

'What is it?'

'I have a plan.'

'What plan?'

'We can do what we did with the fish in training,' Matías explained. 'When the zeltogs come towards us, we should bat them away with the palms of our hands. We just need to watch out that we don't get bitten.'

'Why don't we keep on going with the swords?' asked Martina.

'Well, we've killed about thirty. If the rest all come for us at once, we won't have time to defend ourselves. We only have one sword each, but we have two hands.'

'What if they come at us from behind?'

'Didn't you notice, they're working like an army? They'd have to regroup and then attack again.'

Martina looked thoughtfully at the zeltogs. She put her sword away. She had no idea when they would relaunch their attack, but as she saw them starting to approach she lifted her hands up above her waist, ready for them. On her palms, she began to feel rounded bellies, smooth and cold. They catapulted the zeltogs. It was like watching a shower of frogs falling from the sky. Behind Matias and Martina, the zeltogs bounced on the ground, stunned.

She had no idea how much time had passed. She didn't feel tired at all. She hadn't even noticed that Matías and Socrates were beside her. Suddenly the shower of frogs stopped. The path was clear again. The shapes and details of the place came back to life. She could now hear Matías and Socrates, who had effectively covered their backs. She looked behind her. The zeltogs were trying to reorganize themselves, but it was like they were drunk.

Martina exchanged a glance with Matías. His face was sweaty, but he was all right. He looked at her more seriously than before.

'What now?' asked Martina.

'We get out of here as fast as we can!'

And without waiting for a response, he grabbed his

poncho, dashed over to his horse, clambered on top and fled at a gallop. The zeltogs watched him, stupefied. Martina stood there frozen for a few seconds without knowing what to do. Then finally she reacted. She raced over to her horse and flew like a shot after Matías, with Socrates by her side.

For better or for worse, they were a team now. The three of them. They might not be pals, best friends or anything like that, but they could certainly work together, that much was clear.

Sixteen
Prisoners

Over the next few days the rain eased off, but the sky remained grey and overcast. It was growing colder, and Martina noticed they were moving away from the River of Dark Waters. They no longer heard its comforting gurgle alongside the path.

They advanced, step by step, as the Path of Life snaked through the forest. The wind blew at them from in front. Even Socrates stopped running ahead, instead walking with his head down, muzzle to the ground.

They had begun to climb a gentle incline, one that was becoming increasingly steep. The fresh air and the breeze made the forest seem to breathe like a living animal. The chink of sky they could see overhead was still the same, grey and leaden.

Then, after two days of travelling through similar-looking surroundings, the path suddenly ended on a cliff edge. The soft, dark earth, sludgy and heavy, simply stopped. The vegetation disappeared too and above them opened up an enormous grey sky, like a huge cement vault.

A green-blue river ran some fifty metres below them. The fast-flowing waterway must have been at least twenty metres wide and was blocking their route. To get to the other side they would have to cross a bridge – a rope bridge, with worn cables and rotten slats that didn't look like it would hold a baby zeltog without breaking in half. A couple of poles held the bridge up at each side, while two ropes formed the 'rails' along each edge, with two more holding the wooden slats above the abyss. The wind rocked the bridge and the cables seemed to beg for mercy with each gust. Socrates reached the start of the bridge, sniffed it and backed away, his tail between his legs.

'Now what?' asked Martina. 'You're not thinking of crossi–'

'Of course we're going to cross it,' said Matías.

'Erm, where's the helicopter?'

'At least we have a bridge, so we don't have to walk through thin air.'

'Bridge? One of those solid things, you mean, made from concrete and metal, right? The sort of thing *normal* people use to cross a river or a ravine. Where's that then?'

Matías tested one of the poles with his hand. It didn't feel very firm.

'I don't like the idea of crossing here either, Martina . . .'

'Perfect, so let's not cross it then.'

'. . . But we have no choice.'

Socrates was watching Matías closely and he let out a whimper.

'Don't you see?' said Martina. 'Even a dog can tell that if you add just two grams to that . . . that *thing*, it'll collapse.'

Matías weighed it all up in silence before shaking his head.

'We'll have to leave the horses behind,' he said.

'Yeah? And then how will we travel?'

'Well, I thought we could catch the number sixty bus that passes just down there . . . *We'll walk*. Or do you have a better idea?'

'I can't walk all day! I'm shattered just from riding. And anyway, don't we need the horses to be able to escape in an emergency?'

'Hmm.'

'So?'

'So, nothing. We'll see, as and when it happens.'

Matías dismounted and began to unsaddle his horse, removing what he needed for the journey ahead, the things he would now have to carry himself. Martina watched from horseback.

'There's really no other way to go? To avoid the river?' she asked.

'Avoid the Lipax River to reach the Mountain of Destiny?' Matías said, smiling to himself. 'That's like avoiding the Atlantic to get to Europe.'

'Can't we cross further down there, with a boat or a raft or something?'

'This whole area is full of slave traders. They have their camps all around here.'

'Ugh.'

They released their horses, who cantered around happily, relieved after a long day's work. Martina couldn't help but have a tight feeling in her chest as she watched them trot away.

'They'll be OK, won't they?' she asked.

'Of course they will,' Matías replied.

The sky looked more threatening than ever, and the wind tugged at the ropes, pulling their fibres loose with every gust. The Lipax River roared like a choir of lions.

'Is it very deep?' asked Martina.

'Some sections are. Others aren't, but there are rapids,' responded Matías.

Martina looked across to the riverbank opposite, where the bridge ended. The bank rising from the water was made of rocks and earth. She calculated that the flimsy bridge was twenty metres long. What was that? Seventy footsteps?

'Who's going first?' she asked.

'Let's go together,' Matías replied.

Martina looked at Matías like he'd gone crazy. 'If we do that, we'll be putting more weight on the bridge.'

'My mission is to protect you. I can't do that if you're on that side and I'm over here. Or the other way round.'

'But it won't hold us if we go together.'

'Don't look down and hold on tight to the ropes. Spread out your body weight. That way, if one of the slats gives way, as long as you're holding on, you'll be fine.'

Along with the wind now came the first drops of cold rain, small and sharp like spikes. Martina nodded and turned back to the bridge. She grasped hold of both sides and took a deep breath. The ropes were coarse and bits of them crumbled away like the crust on a loaf of stale bread. Martina placed one foot and then the other on the first slat. She felt like she was on a boat in the middle of a storm.

'Don't look down and walk slowly,' Matías's voice instructed from behind her. The wind was hurting her ears, the rain was stinging her face and she had to squint to see anything.

They began to walk slowly across the bridge. Each step took an eternity. Martina was suddenly grateful she was light. Five, six, seven, eight, nine, ten steps. Then she suddenly remembered someone she had forgotten.

'And Socrates?'

'Martina, don't stop.'

'But what about Socrates?'

'We're halfway across the bridge, Martina! Don't start asking that now!'

The dog was watching them from firm land. He was sniffing at the bridge, unable to decide whether to follow them. His ears were flat against his head.

'But he's my dog. I can't just abandon him!'

'I told you not to bring him. He can wait until we're on the other side!'

Martina peered over Matías's shoulder at Socrates. The animal met her gaze. Just then they heard the first crack.

At first Martina didn't associate the sound with anything in particular, but then she felt herself falling, and she realized the crack had come from the wooden slats right beneath her feet.

She screamed and, in desperation, hugged on to Matías, who did all he could to hold on to her with his one free hand.

'Martina, don't let go of the ropes!'

'Aaaaaggghhh!' was all that Martina could articulate. She looked down and saw the two pieces of wood fall below her. It was a long drop. The slats disappeared into the torrent of water.

'The ropes, Martina, hold on to the ropes!'

Her legs were dangling in the air.

'The ropes!' roared Matías.

Martina reacted. She grabbed on to the cables, pulled upward and, with Matías's help, heaved herself back up on to the nearest remaining slat.

And now, over the sound of the wind, she heard Socrates barking. Martina's head was spinning; she felt seasick. She looked at her dog.

'Socrates, stay there!' she begged him.

But Socrates had overcome his fear of the bridge and bounded on to it. The structure shook like there was an earthquake, and Martina and Matías wobbled from side to side. Socrates stopped and stood still, whining. Matías slipped and landed on his knees with a thud that made the bridge creak.

'Matías!' screamed Martina.

She let go of one of the ropes and went to grab Matías by his clothes. Unsure what to do, Socrates looked behind him and then at Martina, afraid to continue in either direction along slats that were as slippery as a bar of soap beneath his paws. Eventually Matías managed to clamber back to his feet, his face right next to Martina's. If one of them had moved their heads slightly, she thought, they would have kissed. But this wasn't exactly the right time for romance. At that very moment the handrail rope to her right gave way. It did so without much noise; it simply jerked, whipping the air a couple of times before disappearing from sight.

The bridge lurched to one side. Socrates leaped backwards on to the riverbank, just in the nick of time, but Matías and Martina were too far across to retreat. The snapped rope – the one that had disappeared from view – slapped against the riverbank opposite and dangled there like a dead snake.

'Hold on tight to the other handrail!' Matías managed to yell.

Martina did as he said. Matías clung on to the rope with one hand while holding on to Martina with the other. They didn't have much time to think as the remaining handrail immediately gave way. They sank to their knees on to the slats beneath them, but Matías slipped and was left hanging over the side, with Martina now lying down, clutching the wobbling floor.

Suddenly the two ropes holding the wooden slats also snapped. There was nothing to hold them up. The bridge plummeted towards the water.

'Hold o-o-o-on!' yelled Matías.

Martina grabbed hold of the first rope she saw. Matías did the same, clinging as he could to the bridge. Just as she was expecting to plunge into the water, she felt herself being swung with the bridge slats like a pendulum over towards the riverbank, which was now rushing at her like a train.

The last threads of rope, still attached to the opposite bank, swung them along like Tarzan on his vines, only instead of trees there was a wall of mud and stone in front of them. They hurtled into it and after bouncing off, hung there, swaying in the wind. They were dangling in mid-air, but it was better than being in the river.

'We have to climb,' shouted Matías. 'Like it's a ladder!'

But it seemed as if the bridge had heard these very words, and the last ropes holding the bridge up snapped. Martina glanced towards Socrates, who was watching them with an expression of astonishment from the other side of the river. The dog hared off in the other direction, away from the river. Then she felt Matías's hand searching for hers. She didn't let go until they hit the water.

In a heartbeat, the world changed. It turned colder and darker. Water shot up Martina's nose, making her face and head hurt, and the blow yanked her hand away from Matías's.

She may have lost Matías, but what she didn't lose was

her ability to remain calm. She followed the directions of the bubbles as she searched for Matías. She saw him, five or six metres beneath her. Despite her burning lungs, she stopped trying to go up and kicked to go down instead.

The current was strong. It dragged them along, bumping over the sharp rocks on the riverbed. She concentrated on Matías and soon he loomed closer. He gestured with his thumb to go up, and Martina nodded.

Each raindrop hit the water like a tiny bullet penetrating a grey background, and circles of ripples spread across the surface. Martina and Matías burst out of the water, panting for breath as they were swept downriver. Now they had to reach the riverbank. They struck out on a diagonal, trying to go with the flow of the water rather than fight it, until they reached a sandbank protruding into the river. They hauled themselves on to it, crawled to the riverbank and then lay on the ground to rest and regain their strength, panting and blinking the river water from their eyes. They were soaked, but they still had their bags, swords and – what seemed like no mean feat – their lives.

Just as they began to think they had survived their ordeal, they opened their eyes fully and realized they were surrounded by a dozen dirty, dodgy-looking men, dressed in rags. Several of them had scars running across their faces, tattoos on their arms, and they carried swords and knives.

Martina and Matías leaped to their feet and made to try to escape, but they were well and truly surrounded. Resistance was completely futile. Martina saw two individuals take a couple of steps towards them, smiling.

'Well, well, well . . .' said one. 'It seems there are new fish in the Lipax today.'

One wasn't that tall. He had a thick, reddish beard that ended in small braids. His large ears had several earrings. There was also a taller, lankier blonde guy with a tattoo below his throat. 'Real grit', it read. Martina recognized them instantly. She also remembered their names: Aton and Svarko, the two slave traders who had tried to kidnap her after she had spoken to Bernarda in The Crazy Skull.

Seventeen
During the night

There were nine slave traders in total, including Svarko and Aton. They seized Martina and Matías's saddlebags containing their food and blankets, as well as their swords, which were then 'officially confiscated'. Svarko and Aton seemed to think they were in line for the lion's share of the loot.

'We saw 'em first!' moaned Aton, his face red on top of his 'real grit' tattoo.

'And what's more, we paid one hundred coins for that little rat!' added Svarko, pushing the others out of the way with his short, chubby arms.

'Who's the little rat?' asked Martina in a low voice. 'Me?'

'But you buffoons let them escape!' answered another, dressed in a purple velvet jacket which had probably been good and expensive a few years ago.

'Aw, shut up, you dimwits. A little boy tied you in knots!' laughed another. He was probably the cleanest of the lot – which was not much to say – with a handsome face and sweet eyes.

'Excuse me, Sprinkles, did you just tell me to shut up?' asked Svarko.

'Really, give us a break,' said Sprinkles, the relatively clean guy. 'We've got more important things to do.'

'It really annoys me when people tell me to shut up, you know? That's really rude,' insisted Svarko.

'Yeah, whatever.'

'Also, who did you call a dimwit?' said Svarko.

'And anyway, who said you could keep the boy?' interrupted another voice, a trader with long, grey hair tied in a ponytail. 'You didn't pay for 'im!'

'You know how it goes, finders keepers!' insisted yet another trader, Martina didn't know exactly who. 'You lost him!'

'Claiming the boy without ever having caught 'im?! This I have to see!' insisted the one with the ponytail.

Svarko continued to look at the one with the sweet eyes. He swallowed and his 'real grit' tattoo moved as well.

'Hey! Sprinkles! Yeah, I'm talking to you. Who are you calling a dimwit? I asked you a question!' shouted Svarko.

'You! Who else?!'

'Say it again, if you dare. Go on, say it!'

'Dimwit, dimwit, dimwit, dimwit! Happy now? Now, please do shut up, will you?'

At this point Svarko stopped using words to resolve the conflict: he pulled back his fist and pounded it into

Sprinkles' handsome face. Sprinkles was unprepared for the blow but managed to stay on his feet and decided, despite his charming and sweet name, that it was time to forget about being charming or sweet and responded by raining blows and kicks on to whatever was in front of him.

'Martina . . .' said Matías.

At first she couldn't hear him because she was so absorbed in watching the fight.

'Psst . . .'

Martina spun round. Matías beckoned her towards the forest, hoping to make a getaway while the men were distracted by the brawl. However, they had barely taken a step when the traders turned and glared at them.

'Stop right there!' barked Aton.

'Where do you think you're going?'

'I think it's time we took them to camp,' said Aton, walking towards them and grabbing them.

On that point at least, the traders *could* agree. So, they took Martina and Matías through the forest, bundling them along without ceremony, as they continued arguing about who was or was not a dimwit.

Their camp was a wooden bunker with several rooms, deep in the middle of the forest. The building was hidden by the undergrowth and if they hadn't been taken there by the men, Matías and Martina would never have found it.

To get in, they had to enter through a door guarded by scruffy-looking men, similar in appearance to the ones who had caught them. Inside, grime and disorder reigned. Leftovers from meals were scattered across the floor, where several traders lay either sleeping off their most recent drinking session or preparing for the next one. It smelled rank and the walls were stained with marks whose origin Martina didn't even want to guess at. A few flaming torches were all that lit the place, which made it seem even dingier.

The traders shoved the pair into a cage containing at least four other people. They were all thin, filthy and pitiful. Without any further ceremony, the traders locked the cage and walked off, without looking back. The sound of metal against metal echoed in their ears, like the announcement of something definitive. The echo bounced off the narrow walls and quickly faded away. Martina realized she was holding her breath. Not even in her worst nightmares could she have ever imagined anything like this.

And now what? she wondered. She exchanged a quick glance with Matías and then scanned the place where, incredibly but undeniably, she was now a prisoner. Everything was dimly lit and there were no windows or doors beyond the metal bars. The cage walls were made of hard wood, mouldy and marked by the passage of time, but they were solid. Instinctively, she grabbed one of the metal bars, which was much colder than she had expected, and tried to move it. It didn't budge, not even a millimetre. They were truly trapped. With no possibility of escape.

She almost felt like breaking down and crying right then and there, but Matías looked at her calmly, stopping her without needing to say a word. Martina turned toward the rest of the people who were also imprisoned there. There were five of them, and from their condition it was obvious they would be sold as slaves too. For Martina, it was particularly horrifying to see a boy who couldn't have been more than six years old. That sight killed her desire to feel sorry for herself or to cry. If that little boy was there, facing whatever was coming, so could she. Plus, she had Matías with her. Martina realized that if she wasn't with him, she probably would go mad in there.

Meanwhile, Matías took a couple of steps forward into the cage, nodded toward the other prisoners as a form of greeting and sat on the dirty floor, against a wall, where he seemed to calmly wait for something. Martina couldn't guess what it was. And although the idea of doing the same – just sitting down and waiting – seemed unbearable to her, on the other hand Matías was right. They couldn't do anything at that moment. Only wait. Martina almost felt as if she and Matías were saying that to each other at that very moment, even if their mouths were shut. Matías looked at her again, and Martina was certain they were both thinking the same thing. She took a deep breath and, although her mind raced with thoughts, decided to focus on the boy. Maybe she could help him feel better . . . and in doing so, make herself feel better too.

Martina smiled at the boy and asked, 'What's your name?'

'Cyclone,' he replied quietly.

What a name! thought Martina. She then spent some time playing with him. There wasn't much to play with, really, other than a few pebbles and lots of imagination. She tried to tell him stories and soon realized it was not what she did with him or told him that made Cyclone feel better, but her intention to do so. The kid was consoled by the fact that she was trying to comfort him. It was good for him, and also good for her, because it was distracting. It was just fine to keep her mind busy. She was more scared than she dared to admit. She was a little frantic, actually. The idea of being in an unknown world, held captive by slave traders and with no idea of what was going to happen next was more than she could rationally handle. She wanted to avoid thinking too much about it, but couldn't really get it out of her mind.

In between playing with Cyclone, Martina tried reasoning with the traders. She would have begged them, cried out loud even. The only reason why she didn't do it was because she was certain Matias wouldn't approve. They either laughed at her or mocked her, or else stared through her with expressions of immense boredom on their faces. Feeling increasingly desperate, the only thing that kept Martina together was the fact that Matías was silent and showing no fear.

'What now?' she whispered to him eventually, when the traders were distracted.

'We'll have to wait,' he replied.

'Wait? Wait for what?'

'I don't know at this point.'

'What if they actually sell us? Have you thought about that?'

'Of course I have.'

'And?'

'Well, they're not close to any city or town where they can actually do that, so they're going to have to transport us. We won't be stuck in this cage then. And they'll mess up sooner or later, you'll see.'

'What if they split us up?'

'Already afraid you'll miss me?' said Matías, smiling.

Martina was about to answer when she realized he was kidding and kept her mouth shut. She wondered, though, what exactly she would've said. And whether she would've been honest or simply continued their verbal fencing.

At that moment one of the traders entered the room that surrounded the cage, so they stopped talking and waited until he had gone.

'They won't split us up,' continued Matías when the coast was clear. 'That would only complicate things for them. It'd double the job. This isn't the end of anything, Martina. It's only a setback. Just don't start being negative. We need to be ready. We need to fight back when the time comes.'

As night fell they looked out of their cage and assessed the situation. Matías had already checked the metal bars, which were made of iron and very solid, so they knew they couldn't break through them. Outside the cage, the traders, for now, were ignoring them. A cloud of flies buzzed above the murk that covered the only table, where the key to the cage lay among the knives, blades, maps, leftover bread and broken bottles that littered its surface.

'I'm cold,' Martina said to Matías.

Their clothes hadn't yet fully dried and it was still raining outside. Cold air filtered in through gaps in the bunker's walls. Martina shivered and her belly rumbled.

'How are we going to get out of here?' she asked.

'I told you: I don't know, Martina. We're just going to have to wait and take any opportunity we're given.'

'How many men are there?'

'I've counted twenty-seven so far.'

'It's all my fault. If only I hadn't called back to Socrates.'

'That bridge was going to give way anyway. It wasn't your fault. And besides, you didn't call to him. You told him to stay.'

'But if I hadn't tried to talk to hi–'

'Forget about it. We'll get out of here . . . somehow,' Matías interrupted.

The traders had stacked Martina and Matías's swords in one corner, a few metres from the cage. They didn't exactly know what to do with them. They bickered over whether they should be shared between two people, sold, or one person should get to keep them both. In addition to arguing, all of them were shouting and drinking. One of their other favourite activities seemed to be punching each other – laughing all the while – before falling into a drunken heap.

Outside, visible through the open door, a few of the men had made a fire that was protected from the rain by a tarpaulin. Several pots and pans had been placed on the fire and were filled with pieces of sizzling meat and fat, the smoke from which filled the air with a rancid smell.

'Why are there slaves in Novrogod?' Martina asked Matías. 'Isn't it forbidden?'

'There weren't any before, but Voraz allows it now. Officially, only he can decide who will become slaves – mainly those who stand against him – but there are others who take advantage of the situation. Like these traders.'

'So Emelia . . .?'

'What?'

'You saw the Village of the Crescent Moon was destroyed, right?'

'I saw that when I came, yes.'

'What do you think happened with her?'

Matías sighed. 'I don't know, really.'

Martina took a second before she spoke again. 'You don't think she's . . . dead or anything, do you?'

'No.'

'How do you know?'

Martina wasn't sure she wanted to hear this answer, because she felt pretty certain there was no way for Matías to be completely sure.

'A thing like that is quickly known.'

'Do you think she might be a slave, then?'

'Emelia is too good a prisoner to waste on being a slave.'

'And everyone else who was with her?'

Matías shrugged. He was probably too practical to worry about things he couldn't change. He always focused on the problem at hand. Martina decided he was right, in a way. There wasn't much they could do about Emelia at that point.

Through the main entrance they could see the party going on. The traders drank continuously and ate like pigs, pinching food from one another, dropping it on the floor, picking it up again and eating it all the same.

At least that's cured my hunger, thought Martina.

Just at that moment they heard the first cries. These weren't part of the fun and games. These were screams of fear.

'Grab your weapons!' yelled a voice, audible above the confusion.

A screeching sound cut through the din. Martina had heard it before. It was the same noise as the one she had heard that day in Novrogod when she had first met Emelia in the Village of the Crescent Moon.

Eighteen
The horseman

'Tugs,' murmured Matías.

'*What?*' asked Martina. She remembered the agile, swift creatures she had seen in the Village of the Crescent Moon. 'Here?'

The other prisoners gathered around to listen.

'Voraz's army,' replied Matías. 'A patrol. They must have found the camp.'

They heard the clash of swords, along with groans and insults. They couldn't see much through the main door, only a fleeting glance of fighting bodies. Martina grabbed on to the metal bars of their cage.

'Will they release us?' she asked Matías.

'Who? The tugs? Don't make me laugh,' he replied.

'Why not? We haven't done anything. They don't even know who we are.'

'They'll still take us to Voraz and he'll turn us into slaves.'

A trail of grey smoke floated in through the doorway, concealing the battle beyond, and a bitter smell penetrated the camp.

'What's burning?' asked Martina.

Martina and Matías looked at each other. For a moment everything was silent and then they heard a short, dry thud on the roof of the bunker: an arrow embedding itself in the wood. Soon a tongue of fire was licking one side of the doorway. The fire had found a path to devour and it was making its way inside the bunker.

'Matías . . .'

He didn't look at her.

'We have to get out of here,' she continued.

The fire was burning nearby, and the thick, dark smoke reminded Martina of the Wanderer in the Darkness. They all began to cough, their eyes streaming.

'If only we could reach the key,' said Martina.

'The world would just be perfect then, wouldn't it?'

The key lay untouched on the table. Cyclone was crying and the two women were trying to comfort him while the two men watched the fire slowly creep towards them. Matías tugged and pushed at the bars, but the metal wouldn't budge. He yelled in frustration and kicked the bars.

It was then that Martina saw them: two yellow dots gleaming through the smoke. At first Martina thought they might be sparks, but when she saw them move together her pulse quickened.

'Socrates!' she shouted.

'Socrates?' asked Matías. 'Your dog? Here? He can't be.'

'Socrates!' shouted Martina again. 'Here, boy!'

A bark replied, and Martina giggled with happiness.

'Socrates, over here!'

'Socrates, here doggy,' chimed in Matías.

Socrates entered the room. He wagged his tail when he saw them and wasted no time in running over to the bars to say hello to his friend. Martina reached out, grasped the dog's face in both hands and scratched his head while he licked her hand and jumped his front paws up on to the bars.

'Socrates, hello, hello. How did you find us, hey boy? You clever dog.'

'Socrates,' said Matías. 'The key, Socrates! Fetch the key!'

Martina raised her head and saw the fire approaching. By now nearly all the traders had disappeared. They didn't have much time. Any minute now Voraz's tugs would storm in and find them.

'Socrates,' Martina said to the dog, their eyes locked. 'Key. Fetch.'

She accompanied the last word with a gesture towards the table, but Socrates only had eyes for Martina, his front paws still resting on the bars.

Martina pointed to the key again.

'Key, Socrates. On the table. Key.'

Socrates didn't move. His only response was a bark, his tail wagging furiously.

'Key, Socrates. Key.'

Nothing. He just stood there, his back to the table. Martina threw her head backwards.

'Key,' she said sternly, using a commanding voice.

But all the dog did was lick her fingers.

'Great. He would have to be a stupid dog,' said Matías.

'He's not stupid,' replied Martina, annoyed. Socrates barked angrily at him.

'Yeah yeah, woof woof,' answered Matías. 'I know you want to eat me, but if you want to do that, you'll have to fetch the key first, buddy.'

Just then a tug appeared in the doorway. This was the first time Martina had seen one up close. It was two metres tall, its face masked by the shadows. It was dressed in black leather and its head was bald and sunk in its shoulders. It was solidly built and its limbs were powerful, with long arms, like a monkey's.

The tug opened its mouth and screeched. Everyone in the cage shrank back. Just then one of the traders attacked the tug from behind and it turned and went outside to fight. Matías and Martina looked at each other, and then at Socrates, whose ears were now pinned flat back to his head.

'To think he could fetch all those sticks you chucked for him,' remarked Matías.

An idea struck them both at the same time. They looked at each other again and read each other's mind.

'If Socrates thinks the key is a stick . . .' started Martina.

'Then he'll go and fetch it,' concluded Matías. 'But how do we get him to do that?'

Martina removed one of her boots and waved it around in front of Socrates.

'Hey Socrates, look what I've got.'

The dog reacted. His ears pricked up and his gaze moved from being fixed on Martina to looking at the boot. He barked.

'That's it. You like playing, don't you, boy?'

Martina raised her arm to throw the boot.

'Don't miss,' muttered Matías.

The boot flew through the air and landed on the table. It knocked a few other things out of their original positions, including the key. Socrates ran towards the boot, jumped up at the table and picked the boot up in his teeth.

As he came back to the cage, the fire was closing in and it was getting difficult to breathe. Martina felt her lungs burning. Time was running out.

'Good boy!' Martina scratched the dog's head. 'This time, fetch the key.'

Socrates turned his head to where the key had fallen. This time he seemed to look more closely.

'Bring me the key,' whispered Martina in his ear.

Socrates had no idea what the word 'key' meant, but he'd got the hang of bringing things to Martina and, contrary to what Matías thought, he was really very intelligent.

He walked over to the key and picked it up in his mouth. Martina was hopping with joy and, as she put her boot back on, the dog kept watching her. He wagged his tail and, obeying Martina's gestures, carried the key over to her. Reaching through the bars, Martina took hold of the key and quickly unlocked the cage. Then, throwing the door open, she and all the other prisoners rushed out.

Matías made straight for the wall of the building and picked up his and Martina's swords, using an empty sack snatched up from the ground to hold the handles, just in case they were hot from the flames. This done, they ran through the smoke towards the exit.

Outside, a dense rain was falling. They could hear the raindrops hitting the leaves on the chestnut and ash trees as well as the scorched earth. The fire was crackling, and the blackened ashes sizzled. Other than that, though, silence tightened the air in the surrounding woods. Matías dropped the sack and grabbed the swords by their handles, using the rain to cool them down. Martina looked all around. There was nobody in sight. She was surrounded by four walls of smoke and the rain fell like a great grey sheet on the darkness of the night. She felt disoriented and lost.

Matías also peered into the dark. The rain beat down on their heads, pouring down their faces. Martina knew what he was thinking: he was expecting an enemy to appear out of nowhere, and he wanted to be ready for them, to see them before running them through.

'Where is everyone?' asked Martina. 'The battle can't be over already.'

'Maybe they all ran away because of the fire.'

She saw Matías swivelling his head in all directions.

'Matías, we have to go!'

'I know, but I don't know which way is out!'

One of the prisoners interrupted them. He was a tall, slender man aged around thirty, with long hair.

'This way, this way!' he urged.

Matías didn't lower the swords. He offered one to her, but she shook her head. It was dark and foggy. Visibility was limited. She didn't want to risk hurting the wrong person. Cyclone, for example. Matías, once again, seemed to understand without the need of words and after a moment's hesitation he nodded to Martina and set off along the path indicated by the man. Just as Martina was about to follow she glanced back for her dog. The animal had turned towards the opposite direction.

'Socrates!' she called.

The dog didn't appear to have heard her. His body was tensed and he was looking the other way. Martina walked towards him.

'Socrates! Come on, let's go, Socrates!' she urged.

Her feet sank into the mud and cold rainwater ran down into her open mouth. She grabbed hold of the dog's neck to try and move him and that's when she felt it, on the palm of her hand: the dog's throat was vibrating with a growl. Martina let go and turned her eyes in the same direction as the dog was looking.

This is a bad idea, thought Martina. *This is a really bad idea.*

Her hair was sopping wet from the rain and streams of water spilled down her body like cold tears. She caught a whiff of something different, distinct from the smell of the smoke and the wet soil.

'Socrates? What is it? What can you see?' she murmured to the dog.

The answer hit her like a thunderbolt. The grey smoke dissolved to reveal a horseman riding a beautiful white stallion with a long white mane. The rider was clad all in black, wearing a monk's tunic and a hood concealing his face. In one hand he carried a sphere-topped staff. The fire in the bunker illuminated both horse and rider, tinging them red.

The horse was enormous; Martina's head wouldn't even have reached its saddle. Its hooves pawed at the earth, tearing out chunks of grass and splashing black mud up its legs. The rain coursed down its short coat, and both it and its rider were enveloped in a robe of smoke, almost as if it were a part of their outfits.

Man and beast rode towards her, then stopped. Martina didn't know if the image before her was beautiful or terrifying. She slipped and fell backwards. She tried to scream. The air escaped her lungs, but no sound came out. She felt his eyes on her.

The horse reared, picking up its front legs. Martina saw its hooves, filthy and covered in dead leaves. The animal remained airborne for several seconds, its front legs reaching out. Martina knew it would land on top of her and she closed her eyes, waiting for the impact. Then the hooves landed, not on top of Martina but on the earth. Black dirt splashed her face.

And that was it. The rider spun 180 degrees and left, disappearing like a magic trick. All that remained was the rain and the smoke. Martina sat up and tried to steady her breathing. Socrates trotted over to her and licked her face.

'Martina!' came Matías's voice from behind her. 'Are you all right? What's that on your face?'

Martina ran her hand over her face.

'It's just mud.'

'Are you OK?'

'Yeah . . . Um, yes.'

'Well, come on then. We can't waste any more time.'

Martina followed Matías and, as she went, she glanced behind her. Socrates was trailing them and the raindrops were drilling into the wall of smoke. Other than that, there was nothing to be seen.

Nineteen
The end of the Abandoned Territories

It was a stroke of luck that the other prisoners were able to guide them safely through the Abandoned Territories. The five belonged to a nomadic tribe. Moving continually in large groups gave them an advantage if they ever ran into the slave traders or Voraz's patrols. Their fellow prisoners had been captured one day as they had struck out alone, despite warnings from their friends that they were still too few in number to be safe.

The small party now revisited the tribe's usual camping grounds in turn, hoping to find their fellows there. It took them little more than a day. Once they had been reunited, Martina and Matías were able to eat, drink, rest and take on supplies. The nomads did not have any horses to give them, but once they were ready they guided them back to the Path of Life on foot.

Safely back on the Path, Martina, Matías and Socrates

set off on their quest again under a cloudy, but thankfully rainless, sky. Martina was feeling weary after the last few days and all she could think about was getting home to her bed and sleeping for an entire month. However, she knew their voyage was far from over. She finally understood why Matías never looked back: if you wanted to keep moving forward, you couldn't.

'Something's on your mind,' Matías commented after a while.

'Mmm?' responded Martina.

'Earth calling Martina, is there anyone there? Come in, come in.'

'What is it?'

'I can hear your brain whirring from over here. What are you thinking about?'

'Nothing.'

'Nothing?'

'Yeah, nothing.'

'How can you not think about anything?'

'Just don't think.'

Matías resigned himself to silence. Next to Martina, Socrates trotted calmly on, his head low to the ground. He scanned the leaves off to one side and sniffed the earth.

'It's impossible not to think,' Matías said, almost to himself.

Martina took a deep breath and looked up. She wished the clouds would clear; she missed the blue sky. Matías was right: it was impossible not to think. Or at least it was for her. She was always thinking about something, even if it was unimportant.

Right now, she was thinking about the horseman and the white stallion. Why did he let her escape? Why did he do that? Martina kept walking, although for the first time since she had left home, she had the uneasy feeling they might just be walking into a trap.

The forest on both sides of the path ended abruptly. An area of reddish earth came into view, dry and barren, extending as far as the eye could see. A few boulders the same colour as the ground were scattered here and there. Martina, Matías and Socrates had emerged from the bowels of the forest and were now entering the heart of the desert. The sky had cleared a little and a few of the heavy clouds had disappeared. The horizon had been transformed into a blurry line.

'Where are we now?' asked Martina.

'The Desert of Nothing.'

'How did it come about?'

'The mountain range runs between wet areas and dry ones. We've just reached a dry zone. It's been centuries since it last rained here. This is the driest part of Novrogod. Nothing grows here, absolutely nothing.'

That wasn't all – it was also the coldest place. Martina wrapped herself up to try to keep warm but the wind sneaked in through her layers and chilled her to the bone. Martina turned to Matías and asked, 'How come you know so much about geography?'

'I'm just naturally intelligent.'

'Ha! Well, since you're so *naturally* intelligent, where are we going to find water? And food?'

'We're going to ration what we have. The Mountain of Destiny is right in the middle of the Desert of Nothing. Do you have a better suggestion?'

Martina sighed and stalked off; she was done with talking. A little later, her throat began to feel scratchy. What if she got sick out here? They were far more exposed than they were used to, and they had nothing to shelter under.

They walked on in silence, all three with their heads down, their eyes on the ground to withstand the wind that was blowing straight at them. Martina was astonished by the enormity of the desert, and she missed the constant murmuring of the forest. But they'd finished that part of the journey. It was behind them now.

'Does anyone ever come this far?' she asked.

'No, nobody. Why would they?'

Martina had no response to that.

Darkness fell quickly across the sky, but it was soon filled with white stars behind the wisps of cloud. The pale moon gave off an ashen light. The boulders and the arid land formed a never-ending, rusty sheet. Matías refused to light a fire, as it would be far too visible . . . if anyone else was out there, of course.

'So, are we getting close?' asked Martina as she ate some cold roast meat and bread for supper. She didn't want to complain, but if she was honest, the meat was really tough.

'We'll get there tomorrow, all being well,' Matías replied.

Martina was surprised.

'Tomorrow?'

'Around sunset.'

Martina felt her stomach lurch and writhe like an octopus. This time tomorrow they'd be at the Mountain of Destiny. Their journey would be at an end. They'd have to walk all the way back again, but that was fine. If they'd managed it on the way there, they could manage it on the way back.

'How long is it since we left Kelytong?' asked Martina.

Matías swallowed a chunk of bread. Sideways on, he looked like he had a white halo round him, his own personal energy field. Deep down inside, Martina wasn't sorry to be there.

'Six days,' replied Matías.

'Why are you here?'

'It's my mission.'

'You speak all the time about this *mission* . . . What mission, exactly?'

'To make sure you get there.'

'Get where?'

'The Mountain of Destiny. And so the Prophecy may be fulfilled. I believe this –' he gestured at the surroundings with his hand – 'all that we are doing, our journey – this is something really important.'

Martina sighed and looked around. She saw nothing but flat land.

'What's the Mountain of Destiny like?' asked Martina.

Socrates was lying between the two of them and Matías was absent-mindedly stroking his head. 'I don't know. I've never been there before,' he replied.

From the moment they set off the next morning Martina kept her eyes glued to the horizon. She was anxious to see the shape of the Mountain of Destiny rising up before them. She was expecting the path to lead to a bump, a mound that would grow larger and clearer the closer they came to it.

But there was nothing. Just desert.

'Are you sure we're going in the right direction?' she asked eventually.

'Yeah. It's in front of us. I'm not exactly sure where, but it's there,' Matías said.

Martina felt a stab of doubt. What if Matías was wrong? What if the Mountain of Destiny was actually somewhere else? What if they were lost? Or if the Mountain of Destiny didn't actually exist at all?

There was nothing much to do during the day. The terrain was so even, so repetitive, meeting the sky in a smooth line that seemed always equally distant, that Martina soon had the impression they were not really moving at all. Somehow, the desert became like a treadmill on which she was walking but not advancing. The only change came from Socrates' occasional barking. At first, Matías told him to be quiet, but the dog ignored him, and then Matías gave up on the matter. The barks faded into the distance, swallowed by the desert, and soon Socrates himself seemed to grow bored of it as well. They were tired from the journey; Martina's feet hurt and they both grew silent.

In a way, Martina wished they had something interesting to talk about, but the idea of a conversation seemed like a huge effort. The only sound accompanying them, except for some brief comments, was the one made by the soles of their boots striking the ground and, as hours passed by, dragging in the earth. Even Socrates was quiet, awed by the sight of the desert.

Appearances can be deceiving, Matías had said, and she guessed he was right – he had an annoying tendency to be more or less right, though there was no way she was going to tell him that – but she realized that time could also be quite deceiving. How long had she really been in Novrogod up to this point? It was difficult to estimate. At first, keeping her diary had helped her, but when they'd left Kelytong she'd stopped writing altogether. In any case, even if she had only been in Novrogod a few days, it felt like much longer. Time could be measured by days but also by experiences, and in that sense it seemed to stretch out like a tiger waking up.

Night fell, and still there was no mountain, no hill, not even a small mound or any kind of elevation of land. With the night also came the cold. Its chilling presence was not something to welcome after a long day of walking. The sun sank on the horizon, the moon climbed up the sky and they had to stop where they were, in the middle of nothing.

'Are you sure we're going the right way?' Martina asked Matías again.

'As sure as I can possibly be.'

'That's not very reassuring, if you ask me.'

'I'm just being realistic, and no, I didn't ask.'

Martina snorted. Socrates, who was lying by her side, barked once, as if answering. She hoped he didn't start howling.

'However, it's also true that we're running out of supplies,' continued Matías.

'What do you mean?'

'We can't risk going so far into the desert that it's too late to turn round. Do you understand what I mean?'

She did. She understood. And the prospect made her even colder – outside and in.

'What do you suggest, then?'

'Nothing, really. At least, not right now. But if the Mountain of Destiny doesn't appear sometime soon, which I'm sure it will, but if it doesn't . . .'

'What?'

'Well, what do you think? We'll have to turn back.'

Martina had never really thought of failing. She had feared that idea, especially at the beginning, but Matías had convinced her they would prevail. Not finishing what they set out to do would be devastating. She didn't even want those thoughts in her head; she pushed them away, but they hid in dark corners, as if laughing at her.

*

The following day Matías seemed to have charged his energy levels to a higher state. He made Martina get up, stretch out her muscles and prepare for more walking. Once again, the sun and the few clouds they could see seemed to be the only things moving. But Matías had picked up the pace and even if it didn't feel like they were making much progress, there was now just desert behind them, not the tree-covered territory they had come from, so they must have travelled some distance.

Even so, a few hours passed and yet there was still no change in the landscape ahead.

'What happens if we don't find the Mountain?' Martina asked.

'We'll find it.'

'And if we don't?'

'Don't be such a downer.'

Socrates was, as usual, trotting a few metres ahead of them. At that moment they walked up a slight incline and Socrates raced off. After a hundred metres, he stopped and turned to bark at them. Martina and Matías glanced at each other before setting off at a run to catch up with the dog. Once they reached him they saw what Socrates had seen. Matías smiled happily and Martina's eyes popped and her jaw dropped. Socrates was barking and wagging his tail.

'What did I tell you?' said Matías, grinning. 'Don't be so negative.'

An enormous crater opened up before them and in the centre rose a pyramid. It was made of stone, rust-coloured and smooth, carved to perfection in the shape of giant bricks. The edges of the pyramid were straight, as if drawn with a ruler, symmetrical and precise. It must have stood around one hundred metres tall and measured at least the same along each side.

'So that's why we couldn't see it,' murmured Martina. 'Because it was buried. In a crater!'

'It's a pyramid,' said Matías.

'Yes.'

'It's like –' started Matías.

'The pyramids in the golden cubes!' exclaimed Martina.

'Exactly.'

'It's huge!'

'Martina, may I present to you the Mountain of Destiny.'

Twenty
The Mountain of Destiny

The silence of the place felt oppressive to Martina's ears, and she could hear her own heart pounding. The wind rushed down the side of the crater, sweeping across the open space, and whistling and whirling around the pyramid. Even Socrates stood stock-still staring at it.

'What now?' asked Martina.

'Now we go in.'

'Just like that?'

'Just like that.'

'Where's the Butterfly of Light? Inside?'

'I guess so.'

'Yes or no?'

'I've never been here before. I *guess* it's inside; that's what the Prophecy says.'

And Matías strode off down the side of the crater. It was dangerous; the stones could spill into a rockslide without any warning at all. Socrates glanced at Martina before following Matías, his tail wagging from side to side. Matías scratched the dog's head as it trotted along next to him. *After all that bad feeling, there you go, walking along next to each other like you've been best buddies forever!* thought Martina.

'Boys . . .' Martina muttered, pursing her lips.

She began her descent. Several small pebbles skidded downhill, tumbling towards Socrates and Matías's feet. They both spun towards her, their eyes warning her, *Be careful!*

In response, she gave them an ironic smile.

Once they reached the bottom of the crater Martina looked around. The pyramid was enormous, but there was plenty of space around the edges. *Right,* she thought. *Now to find the way in and locate the Butterfly of Light, if it even exists.* And then there were the small matters of setting aflame the Sword of Fire and confirming (or not) whether she actually was The Sent One. And that wasn't all: she still needed to defeat Voraz. Thinking about it, she didn't feel quite so happy to have found the Mountain of Destiny after all.

They walked along one edge of the pyramid. It was impressive. From where they were now, the tip of it almost seemed to touch the sun. The walls were smooth and perfectly formed, not a dent or a crack to be seen among the bricks. But no way in, either. They reached the end of the first edge and turned left. Martina felt like she was peering up a gigantic slide, but instead of going down, it rose infinitely up.

They rounded another corner. They were now walking parallel to the first side they had walked along, and that's where they found it: a broad staircase stretching four metres wide and climbing at least five storeys to an arch-shaped opening in the wall. Yet compared with the overall height of the pyramid, the staircase seemed small.

'The way in,' stated Martina.

'Yes.'

Matías seemed uneasy.

'What is it?' asked Martina.

'I don't know. It's just all very empty.'

'But didn't you say nobody ever comes here?'

'Yeah, but it's *too* deserted,' said Matías.

'We *are* in a desert, though,' replied Martina.

'But there are no guards or anything.'

'Why do you need guards if nobody ever comes here?' asked Martina.

'Feels a little funny.'

'Is it protected in some way, do you think? Like, magically?'

'I don't know.'

On the one hand it was annoying that Matías was mostly right about things. Yet it was equally frustrating when he didn't know stuff.

'OK, that's it. I'm not going to wait here forever until we have some kind of revelation. I'm tired. Shall we go up?' Martina said.

This time Martina led the way, with Matías and Socrates following behind. They climbed the stone-carved steps, one by one, with Martina counting them as she went. There was no handrail, and dust had gathered in the corners of the steps.

When she reached the top Martina saw a broad, arched passageway, at least four or five times her own height, stretching gracefully into the pyramid. The stone pillars supporting the arched roof were a mottled reddish-yellowish colour and had a smooth surface, without any carvings. They reminded Martina of the skin of an ancient animal. The air that came from inside the passageway was cooler than outside, and it carried a deep scent of stone and earth and the desert. When Socrates and Matías arrived at the top of the stairs, the shadows of the threesome cut into the semicircle of sunlight projecting into the pyramid.

Martina remembered that first day in her Grandma Famke's house when they had paused at the doorway and she had seen her shadow on the worn parquet floor. Here it was again on another, different threshold, only her shadow seemed bigger than before. She even thought she saw minuscule specks of dust floating in the air.

They couldn't hear anything coming from within, or see any light. There was nothing. Absolutely nothing.

'Well,' Martina said. 'Shall we go in?'

She noticed she was a bit anxious.

'Just watch out for booby traps,' Matías said, nodding.

'Booby traps?'

'Of course. You know, the sort of thing to deter intruders. Sometimes they're set up around an entrance.

You walk in, activate some secret device and – *boom* – you end up shot through like a pincushion.'

'Ugh!'

'Or something like that.'

'So, how do we get in then?'

Matías shook his head thoughtfully. 'Honestly? I have no idea.'

Martina went to scold him. After all, his mission was exactly that, *to have ideas*, but the words stuck in her throat. Impatient with the humans' indecision, Socrates had started to walk into the pyramid.

'Socrates!' cried Martina.

But the dog continued walking calmly, without so much as a backwards glance at them. He headed down the passageway, and no booby trap went off. Soon the dog disappeared into the darkness.

'Socrates . . .?' called Matías.

A few barks in reply reached their ears.

'Good,' said Matías after a few moments. 'It looks like the way is clear.'

'You don't say.'

They entered and now, without the wind whistling in their ears, the silence fell even heavier around them. The air inside was still, free from the turbulence outside. They paused as they stepped outside the semicircle of sunlight and into the shadows.

'I can't see anything,' said Martina.

'There must be a way we can walk in here and actually *see* where we're headed . . .'

Matías stepped forward, running his hands along the stone to feel his way as his body steadily disappeared into the darkness. As he walked, the shadows first covered his head, then his torso, and seemed to slowly devour him until only his ankles were visible in the semicircle of sunlight.

'Matías . . .?' Martina said, uncertainly.

A click echoed through the tunnel.

'I think I've found something,' said Matías.

He took one more step and was fully submerged in the blackness inside the pyramid, as if he had dived into murky waters. Martina couldn't see him at all. 'Matías!'

'What?'

'I can't see you and didn't know if you'd fallen into a trap or something.'

'No, I'm fine.'

'What do you mean *fine*? Can you tell me what you're doing?'

'Well, actually, I can't tell you . . .'

'You can't? Why?'

'Because I don't really know what I'm doing, that's why.'

'Are you completely bonkers? You can't start doing things you have no idea what –'

'Actually, I think there's a lever here.'

'You *think* there's a lever?'

'Yes! I guess so. Or do you think everything is super clear here? I'm feeling around.'

'Can you do me a favour and get out of there right now before you get us both killed?'

'We're supposed to enter here, right?'

'Well, I'm not really sure. *You*'re the expert.'

'Then, yep, we're supposed to enter here.'

'Weren't you worried about traps?'

There was no answer for a couple of seconds. Martina insisted: 'What's going on?'

'I'm going to pull this lever.'

'*What?* Which lever?'

'Not even I can see it. But I'm going to pull it.'

'No! No way!'

'Yes, I made up my mind. I'm going to pull this lever until something happens.'

'*Until something happens?* Like what?'

'I have no idea, but if it's here, it's for pulling!'

'Or for you to *think* that, while it's actually a trap!'

'I've already got it and I'm pulling!'

'Can you listen to me a bit and –'

'I'm already pulling! Right now!'

Martina held her breath. In any case, it was too late to run. Whatever had to happen, would. She tried to look inside to see what Matías was doing, but she couldn't make out anything. It was pitch black.

Until, in fact, something started to change. Martina couldn't pinpoint exactly what it was. It was a change that was subtle at first, but then intensified. There was more light. Definitely. More light was projecting into the pyramid.

What? thought Martina.

Soon, the inside of the tunnel could be seen. And

Matías too. He was looking at her, smiling and holding a lever attached to the wall. Socrates was beside him and let out a bark. Martina wanted to be angry, but couldn't really. She was mesmerized by the whole thing.

'And all this light?' she asked.

Matías released the lever and gestured for her to look behind her. Martina turned around and was dazzled. Something, a kind of powerful light source, was emerging from the floor behind her.

'Where did this come from?' she murmured, covering her eyes with one hand. 'There was nothing when we arrived.'

'Mirrors,' Matías replied.

'Mirrors?'

She looked at him once more.

'It's a pretty cool mechanism for lighting up inside here, wouldn't you say? With the lever, you raise the mirror behind you, which sends a beam to another mirror further inside, and voilà, light is made.'

Socrates wagged his tail and looked at them, his ears pricked.

'That's why the entrance is on this side, I guess,' said Matías. 'It faces west, the direction in which the sun sets. I suppose it casts its rays during the afternoon and somehow sends it inside the tunnel. Whatever the case, this must work only for a few hours each day and we were lucky enough to arrive at the right time.'

Martina looked behind her once more, but this time tried to move away from the beam of light. Some slabs in the ground had opened up to reveal an enormous mirror that was now reflecting the light rays around the inside of the pyramid.

'I'm no engineer, but this works . . .' said Matías.

'So, the passageway won't light up in the morning, for example?'

'No, I guess not.'

Socrates' barks echoed off the walls. Martina and Matías jumped and turned to look at him. Socrates, satisfied he had their attention, trotted forward.

Further on was another mirror attached to the ceiling. It too was held at just the right angle to reflect the light from outside, like the inside of a periscope. It cast light downwards, revealing a staircase sunk into the depths of the pyramid.

'A staircase leading down,' commented Martina. 'Why make us go up to start with?'

'Martina, I really have no idea. Hey Socrates, wait up!'

Socrates started down the steps.

'That dog is going to get us into trouble,' Matías complained.

'He saved us from the slave traders . . .'

They both sighed and took the first step down to follow the dog, who turned to look at them from below, still wagging his tail. Matías took out his sword and Martina reluctantly unsheathed hers.

'Right, then. Here we go,' said Matías.

This staircase was much longer than the one up to the entrance had been. It went straight down, steeply. *We're never going to reach the bottom,* thought Martina, feeling a little scared. How many steps were there? Martina had lost count. There must have been at least twice as many as on the staircase outside. The sunlight bouncing off the mirrors guided them deep into the dark belly of the Mountain of Destiny, drawing their long shadows on the steps.

'Matías –'

'Shh. Can you hear that?'

They both stopped and stood expectantly.

'It's a *shhh, shshsh* sound,' Martina said, frowning.

'Water?'

They began walking again, quicker now. Eventually they reached a large circular chamber, illuminated by several mirrors shooting sunrays here and there. The rays rose diagonally up before bouncing downwards again, crossing and flying from one side to the other, like broad yellow laser beams.

Beyond that, the interior of the pyramid was empty. The mirrors hanging on the walls were like gigantic stars. The floor was made of stone and through the middle of the chamber ran a river, its water a light green on the surface but dark down below. It must have been at least thirty metres wide. About two-thirds of the way across, a rocky outcrop emerged from the water, big enough for a couple of people to lie on. On it rose a column of black stone, a metre tall, with a small plate on the top, spotlighted by a beam of sunlight.

'There's a hole up there,' said Martina.

Matías strained his eyes up towards the very highest

point of the pyramid. Right at the top he spotted a hole. Sunlight was pouring through it. The beam of light hit a mirror way up high and bounced off it, down towards the ground, like a spotlight on the plate before them.

'There must be some sort of mechanism that projects the light down on to that plate, whatever the height of the sun,' concluded Matías.

'Did you see that?!' exclaimed Martina suddenly.

'What? What happened?'

'In the water!'

'What was it?'

'I'm not sure. Something grey.'

'Where?'

'I don't know. I can't see it any more.'

They heard a couple of barks. Startled, they spun round and saw Socrates sniffing one side of the wall. Standing out against the stone were some pebbles, each no bigger than a thumb and with a letter on it, like a key on a keyboard. Matías and Martina went for a closer look.

'What is it?' asked Martina.

'It's the alphabet.'

'No, you don't say,' retorted Martina sarcastically.

'Come on, Socrates,' said Matías. 'Move over.'

Matías pushed the dog out of the way and examined the different letters. 'They look like keys,' he said.

'What do you think we have to do with them?'

'There's something written on the wall . . .'

Martina stretched out her hand to wipe off the dust.

'No!' shouted Matías.

But Martina's fingers had already touched the stone. In that same instant Matías bowled into her, knocking her to one side. They both tumbled to the floor, Matías on top.

'Are you crazy? What are you doing?!' yelled Martina furiously.

'Booby traps,' replied Matías.

Martina shoved Matías off without looking at him and turned silently back towards the keys as he sat up.

'Booby traps, schmooby tra–'

Martina stopped mid-word.

'Now do you get it?' asked Matías.

The stone slabs they had been sitting on had drawn back to reveal an abyss from which only darkness emerged. Matías picked up a small pebble and dropped it in. It disappeared, devoured by the shadows.

'I didn't hear it fall,' murmured Martina.

A few seconds later the slabs slid back to their normal positions and the floor seemed as solid as ever.

'What do we do now?' asked Martina. 'There's no way I'm stepping on there, but it looks like there's something written on the wall.'

Matías shrugged. He tapped the ground with his feet and stepped on to the false floor.

'Come on.'

'No way!'

Matías crouched down and blew the dust off the wall.

'You're right. There is something written on here.'

'What does it say? Hurry up!'

'It's a riddle.' Matías groaned. 'I'm awful at riddles.'

'A riddle? I love riddles! Read it out!'

'Oh yeah, I'd forgotten that.'

'Read it out!'

So he did.

Ena had five children, as you know
Not one less, not one more
Nea was the second to arrive
Nae the third to thrive
And if you want to go on
To this you must respond:
What was the name of the fifth one?

'It's an anagram, of course,' Martina exclaimed.

'An anagram?'

'Yes, words that use the same letters. I don't know . . . *listen* and *silent* are anagrams, for example. They are my favourite ones. Nea and Nae contain the same letters, as does Ena. She obviously chose her children's names using the letters of her own.'

'Yes, but in what order?'

Martina took out a piece of cloth and the same pencil she had used in Kelytong.

'There are five children. And Ena. So we have . . .'

Martina stopped talking and started writing:

Mother: ENA
Child 1:
Child 2: NEA

Child 3: NAE
Child 4:
Child 5:

'There are six possible combinations of the letters: ENA, EAN, NEA, NAE, ANE and AEN,' Martina said. 'EAN, ANE and AEN are left.'

'OK . . .'

'Ena had to be following some sort of pattern,' Martina explained.

'Maybe names starting with the same letter go together . . . After all, Nea and Nae both begin with an N.'

'Yes, I was thinking the same thing.'

She wrote in the information they knew:

Mother: ENA
Child 1: E
Child 2: NEA
Child 3: NAE
Child 4: A
Child 5: A

'That would make Ean the first child, right?' said Martina.

'Right.'

Martina added this to the list:

Mother: ENA
Child 1: EAN

Child 2: NEA
Child 3: NAE
Child 4: A
Child 5: A

'Great,' said Matías. 'But we still need to work out the *fifth* name. So what now?'

'Now, Matías, we use our brains. We can't get by just using our swords.'

'OK, OK, I'm all ears.'

Martina thought.

'First come the names beginning with an E, then the ones beginning with an N and finally an A. Ena followed the order in her name all the time. For example, in the case of the names beginning with N, Nea came first because the letter E comes first in Ena. Does that make sense?'

'OK . . . The letter's position in Ena determines the order, yeah . . .' Matías said.

'So, for the two names starting with A . . .' Martina began.

'We should choose E first,' Matías said. 'Since E comes before N in Ena . . .'

'So the fourth name is AEN and the fifth must be . . .'

'ANE,' Matías said. 'The fifth child is Ane.'

'It has to be,' Martina agreed.

'Are you sure? You'd swear the fifth name is Ane?'

'On my life? No. There may well be other possibilities – maybe the mother went off-track at the end and gave the fifth child a completely different name. There could be loads of options.'

'You're not helping. I could do with some certainty.'

'It's an uncertain world we live in,' quipped Martina.

Matías looked at the wall. He was standing as far away as he could from the false floor, just in case. He stretched his sword out towards the stone letters, and just before he pressed the A he turned to Martina.

'If I end up being skewered by something and dying, I just want you to know . . .'

'What?'

'I didn't want to die!'

And without looking back again, he pressed the A, then quickly jumped backwards to protect himself. He looked over at Martina. Nothing had happened. Matías cleared his throat, stood up and positioned himself once again, as far as possible from the false floor. He pressed the missing letters: N, E.

'And?' Martina said. 'Nothing's happening.'

Matías turned towards Martina, who was standing with her back to the river. 'Look behind you,' he said.

Martina twirled round and watched as a metal trapeze descended next to the riverbank. It was attached to some rails up on the ceiling. Matías stashed his sword, walked over to the trapeze and grabbed hold of it.

'What were you expecting?' he said to Martina. 'Rain?'

Martina came over and held on to the trapeze next to Matías.They looked at each other, their eyes locked together.

'Now what?' she asked.

'I don't know.'

Socrates looked at them and whimpered.

'Don't worry,' Martina said to him. 'You stay here. It'll all be all right.'

Without warning, the trapeze began to move, carrying them up and over the river. Martina squealed with surprise.

'Honestly,' said Matías, smiling. 'This trip to Novrogod has been incredible.'

They reached the rocky outcrop in the middle of the river and their feet touched firm land. Then they let go of the trapeze, took five or six paces towards the black column and turned to look at each other again. The ray of sunlight streaming through the hole in the top of the pyramid dazzled them. It was the moment of truth. The Butterfly of Light and the Sword of Fire had to be somewhere nearby.

On the plate lay . . .

'What is it?' asked Matías.

'A cocoon?' exclaimed Martina.

That's what it looked like. It must have been about four centimetres long and was a golden-yellow colour, the same as a silkworm cocoon.

'*That's* the Butterfly of Light?' asked Martina. 'So where's the Sword of Fire?'

'I think you have to do something.'

'Do something? Like what?'

'I don't know, something. *You're* The Sent One. You

must have some idea, don't you? You can't expect me to know everything.'

Martina sighed. She had no idea what she was meant to do. She been thrown into this mess without a set of instructions. She stretched her hand out towards the cocoon.

'What are you doing?' Matías asked her in alarm.

'Something!'

She picked up the cocoon and lay it on the palm of her right hand. It was light and cool to the touch. She lifted her hand to her eyes. That's when she noticed that the worm – headless and tailless – was growing warmer. It definitely was. She wasn't imagining it. The cocoon was no longer cold, but warm. And it was getting warmer with each passing moment.

'Martina . . .?'

Martina didn't reply. The cocoon began to roll over.

'Did you do that, Martina? Did you move it, or did it move by itself?'

But Martina was no longer listening. She was holding the chrysalis on the palm of her hand, and she could feel it breathing. And just like that, a small hole began to tear open from the inside. First to emerge were some tiny, fine black legs, followed by a shiny black body and finally two wings folded in on each other, which unfurled like the sails on a ship once they were released from the cocoon. They were an intense yellow colour, criss-crossed with black veins that created delicate patterns.

Martina couldn't tear her eyes away from the butterfly.

The butterfly seemed to tremble, then it stretched and broke free from the cocoon before it flew up into the air and was lost in the semi-darkness and beams of light. It appeared to be dancing. Martina – still with her hand out – watched as it drifted away. It *was* the Butterfly of Light. Without knowing why, she felt tears prick her eyes.

'Did you see that?' she said to Matías.

'Yes,' he replied.

Just then the water seemed to come to life and surged upward, towering several metres above them. A shapeless grey mass pounced towards Matías and dragged him into the water. His sword clattered on to the rock, leaving no other trace of him behind.

Twenty-one
The Sword of Fire

Martina stood as though paralysed. After a few seconds of calm the water surged again and Matías reappeared, imprisoned by the thick grey body of a boa constrictor.

It must have been several metres long. *Ten, at least!* thought Martina, as she watched the serpent disappear back under the water. It was as broad as Martina herself, and under the water its skin gleamed with a green-blue sheen. It stretched and flexed its fibrous muscles as it squeezed Matías. But not only that . . .

It can't be, thought Martina. *I must be imagining things.*

As her eyes scanned the last few metres of the beast the serpent's body divided into two flexible columns, each one topped by a horrifying triangular head. Its eyes were black gashes buried among the scales, and from each of its two mouths poked a long, grey tongue. The heads moved separately but in coordination with the other, working as a team.

One head seemed on the verge of finishing off Matías. Martina knew that boas weren't poisonous; they squeezed their victims to death. The other head was observing her. It watched for a moment, then dived back under the water. Martina hesitated no longer. She grabbed her sword and plunged into the river.

The water was cold. She couldn't find her footing and the sword hampered her movements. The boa raised itself up, holding a motionless Matías, whose face was pale, his eyes already dead. Martina tried to reach him, but she could barely see anything. She sensed a movement nearby and lashed out with her sword, unseeing and weak against the current.

It was like hitting a rock with a stick; she didn't even leave a mark. As she went to try again the serpent wrapped itself round her arm and dived away, dragging her with it. Martina fought to free her arm, but it was stuck. *Come on, come on, comeoncomeon*. She had to make it back up to the surface. With one last effort, she managed to push her face above the water.

Then it happened. Martina took a breath, and the Butterfly landed on her forehead, its wings sticking to her like paint. She was pulled underwater again, but she hardly noticed. From the upper edges of each wing, two large yellow drops, about a centimetre thick, detached themselves. As if alive, they travelled across Martina's forehead, one drop moving to each side, leaving a liquid trail that transformed into a flexible golden metal that clung to her like a second skin.

The drops continued down to her ears, passed in front of them and then moved down her neck, under her clothes, to her shoulders and down each arm until they reached her index fingers, creating a ring on each. Then two more drops detached from the lower parts of the Butterfly's wings and descended between Martina's eyes, down her cheeks, neck, stomach and legs until they encircled her ankles with bands.

The drowning feeling disappeared; it was like she didn't need to breathe. She felt strong, indestructible. The unassuming steel blade in Martina's hand began to glow, from the hilt to the tip, before bursting into flames. It was burning beneath the water.

It's a . . . sword of fire, marvelled Martina. *Not* a *sword of fire,* the *Sword of Fire.*

Martina moved the Sword towards the boa's body. As before, it was a weak, slow movement, but the flaming blade sliced through the serpent's scales like a knife through butter. *I cut it,* thought Martina in disbelief. *I sliced it in two!*

As she withdrew her sword, the two halves of the serpent thrashed around, turning to ash in the water. Like a fire without flames, the fine grey powder devoured the reptile's body until the boa was reduced to scum, floating across the surface of the river.

Matías was now free and kicking his way upward. Martina felt a wave of relief wash over her. They both swam over to Socrates, Martina still holding the blazing sword and with the Butterfly's wings on her forehead, and clambered out of the water.

'Are you OK?' Martina asked Matías.

Matías lay breathing hard on the ground while Socrates licked his face. He had a few bruises and looked like he might just pass out, but he was alive.

'Yes,' he replied, coughing.

Martina still felt overwhelmed. She didn't know exactly what to say, or even think. It was the sweetest, strangest feeling – like she was flying but there was nothing unnatural to it. Somehow, nothing she could say explained anything. Language was not enough.

'I . . . well . . . it's great you are . . . alive . . .' she said.

She wouldn't have known what to do without him there – that was perhaps something to say, but it required too many words. Her brain was not quite ready to produce them.

Matías grinned and said, 'Yeah, you can say that again. Thanks.'

Martina smiled. 'You're welcome.'

'And just in case you still had any doubts, that thing in your hand is the Sword of Fire,' he added.

Martina looked at it, overawed, as the light in the chamber began to fade.

'The light . . .?' questioned Martina, looking around.

'The sun is setting,' responded Matías, getting to his feet.

The sun's rays grew fainter and fainter until they finally disappeared. The Sword of Fire was the only light they had to guide them. It continued to burn with a silent, wild, almost liquid fire. They looked for the steps. Martina's arms and legs felt strong, more powerful than ever before. She studied the golden metal that covered her – it was flexible, like a second skin. She climbed the stairs, two by two, followed by Matías and Socrates.

When they reached the main tunnel and the exit, the sunset was opening up like a vast red cloak in the sky. They raised the levers Matías had lowered to activate the mirrors and the rocks slid back into place. Martina headed outside, the Sword of Fire still aflame in her hand, and stood next to the outer steps. She felt free as never before.

Then she looked down and saw around forty men dressed in chainmail, bearing fierce-looking swords and sabres.

Twenty-two
An unexpected turn of events

As Martina appeared in the entrance the men brandished their swords. The steel gleamed in the red sunset, and Martina noticed their powerful, muscular arms. Matías, who had also reached the entrance, studied them for a few seconds, then broke into a smile.

'What are you smiling about? Do you know them?' Martina asked.

'They're the Desert People. I didn't tell you about them because I wasn't sure they truly existed,' Matías replied.

'Can we trust them?'

Matías took Martina's arm, the one in which she was carrying the Sword of Fire, and raised it into the air. Below them, the men waved their swords and sabres as they shouted with joy. Matías joined in, yelling at the top of his lungs.

'Yes, we can trust them,' said Matías once the celebrations had calmed down.

Martina was about to reply when the bands round her forefingers and ankles undid themselves and the golden droplets began to make their way back up her body towards the Butterfly of Light. Little by little, Martina felt the extra energy also begin to drain away as the liquid returned to the wings. Then, from tip to hilt, the blade of the Sword of Fire stopped glowing, the Butterfly of Light's wings came unstuck from Martina's forehead, and the delicate creature flew up into the air.

'The Butterfly!' said Martina in alarm. 'It's going!'

'Don't worry,' replied Matías. 'I guess it needs its freedom. But when you need it, it'll return.'

Martina watched it fly away.

'It's so . . . awesome,' she murmured.

'Yes,' agreed Matías.

After hugging them and kissing them on their foreheads and hugging them again, the Desert People started to lead Martina, Matías and Socrates to an unknown destination. All along there was greeting, laughing and shouting within the group.

'I feel as if I'm walking in the middle of a buffalo stampede,' Matías said.

After walking for what was perhaps a little more than half an hour (Martina was a bit lost as far as time was concerned), the Desert People led them to an area that Martina assumed at first glance was nothing more than a desert wasteland. However, just as she was least expecting it, a concealed door opened in the ground, leading them into a network of tunnels cut into the dense, beige-coloured rock.

'What is this place?' asked Martina as they stepped down the carved-out stairs under the light of the torches.

She was answered by a man with a tattooed face and well-trimmed goatee beard who had introduced himself as Cracchi. His powerful build made him look like a buffalo, in Martina's opinion at least. She instantly recognized him as their leader.

'We are beneath the desert,' he replied. 'These are our caves. They are naturally formed from the rocks and have always been here, just like the many underground rivers, such as the one that crosses the Mountain of Destiny. It is thanks to the rivers that we are able to move around and find food.'

So the desert wasn't quite what it appeared. *As always, appearances can be deceiving,* thought Martina.

When they reached the main catacomb, the tunnels opened up into an immense chamber. A peaceful river flowed through the centre. They were welcomed by the glow of candles and torches mingling with the moonlight that filtered through a series of holes in the roof. From the outside the holes were practically unnoticeable, but they let through light and, most importantly, heat from the sun.

The room gradually began to fill with women and children, who emerged from the many tunnels and looked at Martina with curiosity.

'Welcome to the dwelling of the Desert People,' said

Cracchi to Martina and Matías. 'It is an honour to have you with us.'

Martina smiled without the least idea of what she should say or do. Why was it an honour to have her with them? What did they really expect? What did they think she was going to do? As far as she knew, the Sword lit up only when the Butterfly touched her forehead . . . and she certainly had no control over that. One thing was clear: she was getting far more attention than she was used to. Or, at least, more attention from a larger number of people than ever before. It was a different kind of attention, too. Something more . . . deferential, for lack of a better word. Altogether, it was a lot to handle.

'Thank you,' replied Matías, seemingly at ease.

'We know you have had a long voyage. Martina, you are a very special person to have undertaken such a journey.'

'I wouldn't have managed it without Matías or Socrates,' she replied

'Most people would have turned back. You are truly brave – *valiente,* as we would say.'

'Me?' squeaked Martina. 'I'm just Martina.'

Everyone fell silent and turned to look at Cracchi and the girl standing next to him. The leader smiled, revealing his large, straight, white teeth.

'Martina Valiente,' he said calmly. 'That's who you are.'

A while later Martina was dancing, laughing and eating, having even more fun than she had had at the Village of the Crescent Moon. The party went on until late, but as there were no clocks in Novrogod, Martina had no idea just how late. All she worried about was having a good time. And that is what she did.

'Now where?'

Rays of sunlight beamed through the small holes in the roof. Everyone else was still sleeping.

'Now we have to go to Voraz's fortress, which is called the Black Castle,' replied Matías.

'What? Voraz's castle? I thought . . . I thought we'd be heading back home.'

She felt a bit naive after saying that, to tell the truth, but somehow she had thought things would end there. It was easy to predict, though, that they wouldn't. What had she really accomplished up to that point? Nothing. She had, with some help, set aflame the Sword of Fire. That was true. At least that one time. But with that came a responsibility she didn't know how to manage. The burden of it all suddenly weighed on her shoulders.

'He has a castle and it's our mission to reach it,' Matías said.

She still tried to resist. 'But . . . but . . .'

She wanted – she *needed* – some rest. She deserved it. She totally did. Just a few days. Or more than just a few. However, Matías was at that very moment gathering together the things they would need in a sack, particularly food and kerpa.

'Why did you think we were here?' he asked without stopping what he was doing. Not waiting for a response, he said, 'To confront Voraz. And defeat him, of course.'

'I was told I had to set aflame the Sword of Fire. That was all. And I've done that already.'

'The Sword of Fire is the only weapon that can defeat Voraz and release the Wizardry. And only *you* can set it aflame.'

'Did someone mention the Wanderer in the Darkness?' said a voice.

Martina's body turned rigid. The dark figure from her nightmares: the Wanderer in the Darkness. But she had never mentioned those dreams to anyone.

'Cracchi,' said Matías, smiling. 'Good morning.'

'Good morning.'

'What did you say?' Martina said, turning towards the strong leader. He had approached so quietly that she hadn't heard him arrive.

'What did I say about what?' he asked.

'If someone had mentioned who?' asked Martina.

'Voraz, the Wanderer in the Darkness,' Cracchi said.

'Why do you call him that?' said Martina.

'That's what everyone calls him, and it's what he calls himself. *Voraz, the Wanderer in the Darkness,*' replied Cracchi. 'But he ought to be afraid now that you're here; that's what I thought when I heard you mention his name.'

Martina didn't respond. Off to one side, Matías and Cracchi began discussing what they would need for their fast-approaching departure. By now Martina had spent long enough in Novrogod to understand that the figure from her nightmares and the person they were about to meet were one and the same.

She hadn't expected this turn of events, although perhaps it wasn't such a surprise after everything that had happened. *However far you go, the enemies you carry within will always be by your side*, she thought.

'What's this?' Matías asked Cracchi before they left.

It didn't look like much. Just a slender clay bottle, no bigger than a hand, with a cork stopper in the top.

'A bottle left by the Great Wizard,' replied Cracchi.

'What –?'

'Socrates the Wizard, not your little dog, left a bottle of Wizardry for The Sent One to use should they ever require it,' explained Cracchi.

Martina approached as Matías ran his fingers over the surface of the bottle. It was an opaque green colour, its texture rough beneath his fingers. They couldn't see anything inside it.

'There's Wizardry inside?' asked Martina.

'Yes,' answered Cracchi. 'But only a small amount.'

Matías lifted his eyes to look at Cracchi.

'Something wrong?' Cracchi asked.

'Um. No,' answered Matías.

Everybody looked at him. Matías didn't add anything, seemingly deep in thought.

'Are you sure?' insisted Cracchi.

'Yeah. Everything's cool,' Matías said.

Everybody accepted his words with no comment and busied themselves with something else. Martina continued to watch him, though. She tried to read Matías's emotions but couldn't. He seemed submerged in a strange cloud. Normally he showed them – or at least he didn't make an effort to hide them. He was never afraid of being who he was. He had a self-confidence she envied . . . but for now that seemed to have disappeared. Then the moment passed and they continued preparations.

The Desert People presented them with a boat around six metres long with a central mast. There was no doubt about what that meant: the time for goodbyes had come. Martina had another one of those moments where she wasn't entirely sure how fast time was passing. Sometimes it seemed to slow down, sometimes to speed up. The only certainty was that it wasn't easy to adjust. Changes were usually unpredictable, but even when they weren't, even when they could be foreseen, even then, it wasn't easy to be entirely prepared.

Martina had felt protected and strangely at home with the Desert People, unexpectedly cared for and valued by everyone, but especially by Cracchi, who had even given her a name. It was the first time she'd been given a name for something she had done or for something she was about to do. Or, even, for who she actually was. It was a name that surprised her a little but allowed her to see herself in a way she hadn't before.

She would have liked to stay longer. She would have liked the farewell to last longer; she would've liked to talk more, ask more, rest more, but she knew that there was no point in dragging things out just for the sake of it. Everything took as much time as it had to. That was something she was learning.

After briefly saying goodbye to various people, she stood in front of Cracchi, just before getting on the boat. He looked at her with clear, calm eyes and a confident smile.

'Thank you,' Martina said to him. 'For everything.'

Cracchi's straight teeth appeared from behind his lips.

'I suppose it should be the other way around, but you're welcome. It was a pleasure. Come back whenever you want.'

Martina smiled.

'I don't know when I'll come back.'

Actually, she thought, *I don't know* if *I'll come back*. But she hadn't dared to say it. Suddenly, out of nowhere, she felt a lump in her throat.

Cracchi continued, 'Well, when you do, we'll be right here. Let's not say too many goodbyes now because I'm sure we'll see each other again. Here or somewhere else.'

'Really?'

'You're going to do great things. You don't expect me to miss them, do you? Now, there's a boat waiting for you. And also a boy, I should say.'

Cracchi motioned with his chin, and Martina turned to see Matías settling into the boat. Socrates was climbing in too, looking suspicious.

'And a dog,' said Martina.

'Yes, but the one really waiting for you is the boy. I think he's very aware of that. Of the fact that he is waiting for you. Not just for this journey. He knows that he should keep close to you – he's a clever one. About that he certainly knows. As for sailing, well, I'm not so sure.'

'I hope he does because I don't know a thing.'

'Nah, you both'll manage just fine. You'll see.'

Matías was looking now at her. He hadn't heard Cracchi's words. At least, that's what Martina thought. Martina gave Cracchi one last smile and felt ready for the next step. That's how it was. Take a step. Then another. That was always the way and that was how she reached the slightly unsteady surface of the boat's deck. Martina sat at the front, Socrates made himself comfortable in the middle and Matías took up position at the rear, in charge of the rudder.

They set sail, and there was nothing left to do but look ahead. Despite Cracchi's predictions about his navigation skills, Matías seemed prepared, at the very least, to prevent the boat from smashing against one of the walls. He followed the current's direction and guided the boat with a steady hand.

He didn't need any help, and, in fact, Martina preferred it that way. She just needed to relax for a while. To empty her head. Now she had left the Desert People behind, she also missed her own home. She tried to control that emotion, even to hide it, just in case Matías noticed. She remained seated and focused on observing the place.

They floated in silence through long caverns, passing pointy stalactites on their way. It was cool and pleasant; the sound of the water echoed against the rocky tunnel they were travelling through. Every so often, there were small holes in the surface, invisible cracks, where beams of yellow light slipped through, illuminating the water and giving it an unexpected glow. Part of that light was then reflected on the walls, giving an unusual life to the rocky corridor, which seemed to stretch endlessly. If Martina hadn't had other things on her mind, she would have thought it was the best ride ever.

They travelled in silence for hours. As they reached the final cave a bright splendour dazzled them. Having become so accustomed to the dim light, they were forced to cover their eyes with their hands.

The river led out of the cave and to a bright blue sea with foaming white waves. The sky was clear and the sun was shining. Matías directed the boat towards the shore, where the water lapped on to a yellow sandy beach surrounded by dunes. They climbed out of the boat and as they sank their feet into the sand Martina had the feeling that it would be some time before their footprints would be replaced by others. The wind might erase them if it blew, or the rain if it fell, but there were no other living beings here.

She helped Matías secure the boat while Socrates bounded joyfully along the beach, happy to be out in the open once more. The sun wasn't as high as she had thought; it was just the contrast from the semi-darkness to daylight that had impressed her, making her think it was earlier than it really was. In just over an hour, the sun was already low on the horizon, nearing the sea.

They prepared themselves for the following day, which basically meant eating and resting. They both were tired and wouldn't continue their journey until tomorrow. As night fell and the weather grew windier, Matías lay down on the sand. Far in the distance, the sea and the sky met, forming a blurred line as the sun disappeared. There wasn't much to do, really. Martina sat next to Matías, while Socrates ran around the beach, sniffing here and there. They watched the sunset together in silence.

'Voraz's Castle is that way,' he said finally.

'Across the ocean?'

'In the middle of the ocean. It's on the Black Rock where Socrates and Voraz fought their last battle.'

'How do you know?'

'Same as I've known all the other stuff: because I was trained for this.'

'Oh, OK. The Prophecy and all that.'

'Yes. And all that.'

Matías took out some food and drink and passed it to Martina, who took it. She started eating without much enthusiasm but soon realized that her body welcomed the nourishment.

'And has it been the way you expected?'

For a second, Matías seemed confused.

'What has?' he asked.

'All this. After all your training, has it been the way you expected it to be?'

Matías scratched the nape of his neck.

'I don't know. It's been what it's been.'

Martina didn't know exactly what to make of that. She would've liked something more reassuring, but she thought she understood what he meant.

'OK.'

'And for you? Has it been what *you* expected?'

'I had absolutely no *idea* what to expect, so . . .'

Matías let a moment pass by. He then asked, 'You feeling nervous?'

Martina shrugged. 'Why did Voraz steal the Wizardry?' she asked.

'Out of voracity, you know, greed,' Matías said, smiling humourlessly. 'As long as he has it locked away in the Oracle, he is the only one who can use it.'

'What's the Oracle?'

'Nobody knows. Some sort of container for the Wizardry, I suppose.'

'What does Voraz look like?'

'I don't know. They say nobody has ever seen his face.'

'I think I've been having dreams about him for as long as I remember. Well, nightmares, really.'

Matías raised his eyebrows and blew out a long breath.

'What does the Prophecy say about my meeting with Voraz?' Martina asked.

'That you defeat him.'

'Are prophecies always correct?'

'No. And the prophecies themselves warn you about that. The future isn't set in stone. When you decided to come here, the Prophecy began to come true, but you could have decided not to come. That's why Cracchi told you how significant it was that you came.'

Martina intertwined her fingers and squeezed them. Her skin was warmer than usual, though she felt cold inside. There are moments when people face their destinies; perhaps that moment had come for her, though it felt a bit soon. Wasn't she too young for such a thing? On the other hand, who says that a twelve-year-old cannot face her destiny? Maybe twelve-year-olds did that every day without even knowing it. The problem was that this felt bigger than just her destiny. It involved more people, and that was scary. She wanted to jump, scream, run, curl up, sleep – everything at once. She had never feared – really feared – what was to come until that moment.

Matías looked at Martina out of the corner of his eye. He clenched his jaw and stared into the horizon. Whatever had been bothering him before getting on the boat was now behind him. His eyes were clear once more – and full of determination. That helped her.

'What do you think?' she asked him. 'Are we going to defeat Voraz?'

'I hope so.'

Twenty-three
Voraz's Black Castle

The next morning the sky was cloudy. Matías unfurled the sails and they left under a light wind that filled the two white cloth triangles that formed the sails. Martina soon got used to the movement of the waves. The vessel bobbed about on the water and, of all of them, Socrates suffered the most, hunkering down and whimpering.

For several hours they travelled without any problems. The dunes creased into the sea at their backs and the horizon opened up before them. When they could no longer see land, a stiff breeze picked up, which began to rock the boat. The waves knocked the vessel from side to side and Socrates buried his head in his paws.

'There's going to be a storm,' said Matías, gazing up at the clouds.

'A storm? This boat will never survive a storm. Can't we go back?' Martina replied.

'It'll catch us anyway.'

'So?'

Matías grimaced. 'So, we're going straight through the middle of it,' he announced.

The waves grew in size and strength, and the wind swirled around them. They held on tight to the ropes that were tied fast. The rain fell in big, fat drops like pebbles. They hurt Martina's arms and back as they hit her, yet she had nothing to cover herself with. Between them, they clung on to Socrates with one hand each as the boat swayed violently.

'Matías, we have to do something!' Martina shouted.

'I wanted to save this for later, just in case.'

'What? I can't hear you!'

Matías didn't reply. He let go of Socrates, reached into his sack and took out the green bottle that Cracchi had given him.

'What are you going to do with that?' asked Martina.

'I want you to imagine us floating on a calm sea, far away from this storm!'

'Why?'

'Stop asking questions and just do it!'

Matías stood up and held on to the mast as best he could while he tried to pull out the stopper one-handed, but the rain made his fingers slippery.

'So?' asked Martina.

'Keep imagining it's not raining!'

'I've been doing that for a while now. Can't you hurry up?'

'I'm going as fast as I can!'

The boat shook. Matías sat down and they both

wrapped their legs round the mast. Martina tried to hug Socrates into the mast as well. Finally Matías managed to get the top off the bottle and Martina thought she detected the scent of jasmine. Matías was still focusing on the bottle.

'Keep imagining it's not raining!' Matías told her.

She did, and then started to notice that the rain was no longer falling with the same ferocity. Socrates stopped whining and looked up. The downpour on the boat stopped, the wind dropped, and the sea around them flattened out like a mirror. Martina looked about.

'Has it stopped?' she asked.

Matías shook his head. It was still raining but it couldn't reach them; they were protected by an enormous bubble with a multicoloured surface that formed a sphere of about fifteen metres around them. Different tones of blue, purple and red cascaded from above, some shades crossing others, changing shapes, swapping sides and generally floating around them. The waves, the entire storm – everything bumped up against the outside of the bubble.

'Is that the Wizardry?' asked Martina.

'Yes.'

'But how are we going to go forward? There's no wind.'

'Think that you want a breeze,' said Matías, running a hand through his wet hair. 'A gentle one, mind you.'

Martina laughed, and, still dripping with rain, she imagined a gentle wind. The sails swelled as if they were breathing and a current of air propelled them forward.

*

Night was starting to fall when they spotted a dark speck in front of them, through the bubble. The Wizardry seemed to be losing its power and the bubble was becoming more see-through. Their surroundings were clearer now and they could just make out the dot caught between the sky and the water. It didn't look like much, but as they grew closer it grew too, becoming a black smudge in the distance.

'Is it a mountain?' asked Martina.

'I've never been there. All I know is that it used to be an island in the middle of the ocean. When Voraz decided to hide the Oracle there, he turned the place to black rock, and now they say it's nothing more than a lifeless crag rising from the sea.'

It was dark by the time they reached the rock. The Wizardry around the boat had gone now, the colours fading into nothing. The rain had ceased but the sky still looked ominous and flashes of lightning lit up the clouds. The sound came some seconds later, rumbling through the air. *There's nowhere to hide,* thought Martina.

The black stone castle had four tall towers, one in each corner. The front facade had only two windows and the entrance lay some twenty metres above sea level. From where Martina and Matías were sitting in their boat, the building loomed vast and dangerous above them. The silence assaulted their ears and even Socrates had fallen quiet. Their only company was the sound of the waves lapping against the rock.

The tide carried them right up to the rock, the prow

bumping against the castle wall. Martina thought about the Butterfly of Light, the one thing she needed to help her set aflame the Sword of Fire. She wondered where it was and whether its delicate wings had made a similar journey to theirs. She gazed up towards the entrance of the castle and a shiver ran down her back.

'How are we going to get up there?' she asked.

Matías gazed up at the castle walls too. A few of the stones were jutting out from the smooth surface. Not a lot, but it was something at least.

'We climb,' he answered.

'And Socrates?

'I brought a rope. We'll tie him on and pull him up once we get to the top.'

'You sure about that?'

'I'm not going to get this far and be stopped by this. Besides, I've trained precisely for this sort of thing.'

Martina nodded, not entirely convinced, although it was true he was no scrawny teenager. Matías took out a hook attached to a rope from his bag. He swung it up towards the castle entrance and the claw caught on the overhang. Matías pulled on the rope to test it and the metal hook held fast.

'Ready?' he asked.

'No.'

'I thought you said you were getting bored. This has to be more fun than Rodó Park back home, eh?'

Martina rolled her eyes and said nothing. They tied Socrates to the other end of the rope and, leaving him in the boat at the foot of the wall for now, they began to climb. It wasn't too difficult. Martina thought back to those days in Kelytong when she had been made to climb the pole. She had learned something useful after all. The castle wall offered plenty of footholds and, with the rope there to help them, they got off to a good start.

They were about halfway up when it began to rain again. It wasn't heavy, but it was rain all the same. It made the wall slick, wet and more difficult to climb. One of Martina's feet slipped and she slid down the wall, grazing her leg, until her foot found a hold and stopped her fall. Her knee was bleeding.

'Are you OK?' yelled Matías from above.

'Yes!' she called back.

Martina continued to climb. Her hands were burning and her whole body ached. She looked down. Socrates was watching her from the deck of the boat. Then one of her hands touched a smooth surface and she didn't know whether to be happy or terrified; she'd made it to the entrance.

Matías helped her up the last little bit and between them they pulled Socrates up. The rope spun him in circles and he looked around, paddling his legs, until he finally reached the top. He was relieved to have all four paws back on solid ground. Martina scratched his soggy head.

They stood up and turned towards the entrance that was hidden in the shadows. From inside came a blast of warm, moist air, like the breath of a monster. Beneath the rainwater on her skin, Martina broke into a sweat. Her heartbeat pounded in her chest and in her temples. She was trembling, with a mix of anticipation and raw fear. Every muscle screamed to turn back and flee, but she took a deep breath, which made her shiver some more, held the air in her lungs and resisted the impulse to run.

Matías looked at her and she held his gaze.

'You OK?' he asked.

Am I? she wondered.

'Yeah, sure,' she replied.

'We're in this together, you know?'

Martina nodded. There was nothing else to say, really. It was comforting to have him there. That was all.

They took a few steps forward and were swallowed by the darkness.

Twenty-four
The meeting

As if by magic, the torches on the walls burst into flame, a dozen or so on each side. A passageway stretched out before them, the dim yellow light illuminating the way.

'How did you do that?' asked Martina. 'Did you use some leftover Wizardry, move a lever or something?'

'No, I didn't do anything. And anyway, the Wizardry has all gone.'

Martina shrugged and took a step forward into the corridor. They walked until they reached a staircase rising from the stone. They went up, craning their necks and straining their ears. The only sound they could hear, however, was the storm now raging outside.

The staircase curled around like a snail's shell as they continued in what felt like a never-ending coil. They finally reached the top and emerged into an enormous chamber. The ceiling was so high it was lost in the shadows.

There were no lit torches but at that moment a bolt of lightning exploded in the sky. The flash of light illuminated two enormous stained-glass windows featuring pictures of hooded figures and demons. Otherwise, the room was vast and empty, containing nothing more than a large rectangular stone in the centre.

'It looks like a coffin,' said Martina.

They began to move towards it. Given its size, it indeed appeared to be a coffin. Although, on a closer look, it clearly was not. Rather, it was a rock shaped like an enormous box, one metre high, two metres long, and one metre wide. Its sides were straight and sharp. The surfaces were covered in tiny cracks, like the dry desert earth. The stone was dark, the colour somewhere between brown and grey.

'There's something on the top,' whispered Martina.

Matías didn't reply immediately. He paused for a moment, then said, 'You're right.'

It looked like someone was lying on top of the stone, but it was so dark that from where they were they couldn't make out the features. Exchanging a look, they both touched a hand to the hilts of their swords.

They took another step forward, then another, gritting their teeth and studying the dark corners of the room. The unsettling silence inside was barely disturbed by the storm outside. Then, with a few metres still to go before they reached the stone, Matías stopped.

'What is it?' hissed Martina.

She stopped behind him and for a few moments they

stayed like that, until Matías took another few steps forward. Then he stopped again, motionless and silent, blocking Martina's way with his sword.

'Matías, what's wrong?' she whispered.

Another flash of lightning lit up the sky and for a split-second the room was bathed in a pale light. Martina could now see more clearly.

'Emelia?' she murmured.

It was the princess, lying there completely frozen, her arms crossed over her chest. Martina felt the energy in her body drain away, as if she had been unplugged.

'Is she dead?' she asked.

Matías didn't reply, but continued to creep forward until he reached the stone. Silently he examined Emelia for a few seconds, just as a clap of thunder exploded overhead.

'Matías . . .?' Martina said.

She closed the distance between them. What she found was a perfect version of Emelia carved out of rock, lying on top of the stone. Matías pulled out his sword and stepped away. He looked up, as if searching for someone.

'Matías . . .?'

He didn't reply. Instead, a cackle echoed around the darkness.

'What was that?' asked Martina.

Martina now looked up as well, but neither of them could see anything apart from the dense blackness.

'Not *what*, but *who* . . .' said a serious voice that seemed to erupt from all four corners of the room.

That voice, thought Martina. *I know that voice . . .*

Little by little, a shape began to appear, the outline of a flowing cape, and Matías gasped. The Wanderer in the Darkness descended from above until he was almost facing them, hovering some five metres from the floor. He looked exactly as Martina had seen him in the dreams she had had since she was a little girl. He was wrapped in a broad black cape that covered his head and face. In his hand, he carried a wooden staff – as tall as he was – topped with a sphere.

Matías thrust his sword towards the figure, gritting his teeth.

'Undo the curse on Emelia.'

'It's one of my favourite tricks,' Voraz said. 'Turning people into stone. The distance between a rock and a living person is surprisingly small.'

Matías stepped forward and grasped his sword with both hands. He held it poised and ready, but he didn't take his eyes off Voraz, who let out a sigh of impatience.

'Really, Matías?' Voraz said.

Voraz waved his staff and Matías's sword shot out of his hands and hung suspended in the air in front of the dark figure.

How does he know Matías's name? thought Martina. Her brain tried to put the pieces together. She wasn't quite there yet, but something was starting to make sense. Voraz seemed to be studying the sword with indifference. The weapon floated in front of him. He gestured again with his staff – a small movement, very small – and the sword shattered into pieces that fell to the floor like shards of glass.

Matías swallowed, not knowing what to do. Martina was also out of ideas, and she doubted whether she really had much to offer if the Butterfly of Light didn't show up some time soon. But then the penny dropped: she recognized that voice. Her heart leaped. It couldn't be. It was impossible.

'You?' Martina said as she stepped forward. 'Is it really *you*?'

A laugh reverberated off the walls. Several of the torches started burning around the room, which gave the sensation of being trapped inside a huge oven.

'Martina, Martina. I've been waiting for this moment for a long time.'

A hand emerged from between the folds of the cape and lowered the hood. Matías's eyes grew as big as saucers.

'*What*?' he said. 'It can't be . . .'

Voraz ignored him.

'I have to say, Martina, being so good at riddles, I'm amazed it took you this long to work out this most simple of puzzles.'

Zavro looked at them, smiling broadly.

'I don't understand . . .' murmured Matías. He looked like a little boy.

'*Zavro* is an anagram of *Voraz*,' replied Martina.

Zavro – or rather *Voraz* – bowed.

'It can't be,' babbled Matías, bewildered. 'You trained me . . .'

'And I did an incredible job. You made it all the way here, didn't you?'

Matías shook his head weakly. He looked surprisingly calm. Martina imagined she might have been trying to smash Zavro into pieces in his place, but Matías appeared quiet and serene as always.

'Why?' he asked. 'Why did you do all of this?'

Voraz gazed at him calmly. 'Matías, what does it matter?'

Matías's breathing got a little heavier.

'Right before coming here, it surprised me that the Wizard Socrates had left the bottle containing Wizardry to the Desert People. I didn't know what to think about it, back in the moment.' Matías looked at Voraz. 'He should've left it to you . . .'

Martina also started making connections.

'It was *you*,' said Martina. 'The day of the storm, on the white horse. When we escaped from the slave traders in the forest.'

'How else were you going to get away?' said Voraz, smiling.

'That's why Socrates the dog appeared. You brought him to us.'

'The incident with those traders wasn't planned. I had to get you out of there, but I couldn't get my soldiers to just release you, and I couldn't exactly walk in there myself, now, could I?'

'And you planted the zeltogs in our way.'

'I had to test you.'

'Why? Why go through all of this?'

'So that you would set aflame the Sword. Why else?'

'But . . . why? Why are yo–?'

'Martina,' interrupted Matías. 'This is all a trap. Everythi–'

His voice broke off. Voraz had waved his staff again and Matías froze, open-mouthed, where he was standing. He had been turned to the same cracked, grey-brown stone as Emelia.

'Matías!' screamed Martina.

Socrates took a couple of steps forward, baring his teeth. Voraz waved the staff again and he too froze, a statue of a ferocious dog.

'What did you do?' yelled Martina. 'What did you do?!'

She looked in horror at the two figures in front of her as she shuffled back, distraught.

'Martina –'

'Are you crazy? What have you done?!'

Her head felt like it might explode, her legs and arms felt numb, and she was struggling to breathe.

'I am your only chance, Martina.'

For a moment she felt so disoriented that she had no idea what to do or even how she felt. All she knew – and the recognition hit her so suddenly – was that once again she was stuck in the same old place, where somebody more powerful took over. Where destiny was impossible to control. That's what she was thinking. *Always stuck in the same old place*. When was she ever going to *move*?

'I want to go home,' she said.

The words felt ridiculous in her mouth. She was crying. She could feel the tears on her cheeks.

'Martina, you are home,' Voraz said.

Martina stood there looking at him. She was breathing in and out through her open mouth.

'What?'

'*You* are the answer, Martina. You always have been. You are The Sent One. You and only you can set aflame the Sword of Fire. You are the last remains of Wizardry in Novrogod.' Voraz seemed to be taking her measure with his eyes. 'The only being beyond my control.'

Martina swallowed. Her knees trembled, her teeth were chattering and a cold sweat covered her back.

'You want to control *all* the Wizardry? Is that it?' she asked.

'Martina, I did it all for you.'

'For me?'

'So that you can discover who you truly are.'

'But I didn't ask to discover anything!'

'Are you sure? Aren't you fed up with feeling stuck? Of nobody seeing just how special you are? Of them behaving as if you don't even exist? Aren't you fed up with it all?'

Martina didn't know how to reply. She dried her tears and Voraz smiled.

'I think you are,' he continued. 'You're fed up. Fed up with running away. Of constantly hiding. Of feeling like you're going nowhere. First you realized that. And then you discovered that you're special, that appearances can be deceiving, Martina. And that is why you're here.'

Martina didn't immediately reply. Was any of this real? She wasn't in Montevideo, or even Novrogod, but trapped in a grey area somewhere between the two.

A quiet beating of wings fluttered through the air. Martina looked up and Voraz sucked in a deep breath. A pair of yellow and black wings wearily zigzagged towards Martina's forehead, where the Butterfly lay down its fine, delicate wings.

'You see, Martina,' began Voraz as he watched the brilliant golden drops run along Martina's arms and legs before wrapping bands round her ankles and forefingers. 'There are two sides to all of us.'

Martina looked at Voraz in silence, confused. The energy from the Butterfly of Light coursed through her body, filling it with life and strength, and yet she felt unwell.

'But there is always one side of ourselves that we cannot ignore,' continued Voraz. 'And you cannot stop being The Sent One, Martina, even if you tried. Come, set the Sword aflame. It's yours.'

Martina looked at her sword, clueless as to what to do. She shook her head. Her throat was burning, and she felt a knot in it. If she tried to speak, she knew she would start crying again.

Voraz smiled. He did so calmly, his teeth lighting up the room, his eyes clamped firmly on her. Martina saw the person who had been with her in Kelytong. For a moment he was the person who had spoken to her before she set out on the Path of Life.

'It's time to emerge from your cocoon. It's time for you to stretch your wings and fly. It's time for you to be *you*.'

Martina looked at the sword and, after an initial tremble, she saw her hand move towards the hilt as if of its own volition. Her fingers closed round the handle and she grasped it at the same time as her arm lifted it into the air. The cold metal was transformed into a long tongue of fire.

Twenty-five
Martina Valiente

Voraz watched the Sword in flames and his gaze softened.

'It's beautiful,' he murmured.

Martina closed her eyes. She felt like she was on a narrow ledge next to a great drop, just about to fall. She almost believed she could see rocks, like teeth, metres beneath her, ripping into the sea. She had to get a grip of herself. She remembered the last dream she'd had of the Wanderer in the Darkness, the one in which she had finally confronted him. She thought hard and imagined herself floating.

Her feet left the floor. It was as if someone was lifting her by her shoulders. She opened her eyes and saw Voraz was closer. She was now floating three metres off the ground.

'You're a quick learner, Martina,' he said.

Using just her imagination, she was able to move from side to side. Flying like this made her feel almost euphoric and she sensed a flutter in her belly. Goose bumps rose over her body and she sensed a sweet taste at the back of her throat as the air brushed against her face. Finally she turned to face Voraz and held the Sword out as if to attack.

'What?' asked the figure in the black cape. 'What are you thinking?'

She charged at him. He waited for her without moving. When she reached him, she passed straight through him like he was nothing but air. Martina halted and spun back round. Voraz turned to look at her.

'Martina, Martina, Martina. What are you doing? You really want to destroy me? Are you sure? Think about it. Don't you see what I'm doing? I am giving you wings, Martina. I am empowering you, setting you free. Who really has done that for you before? Have you thought about that?' he said.

The thing was *why*. Why was he doing such a thing? Amid the sea of rage that swamped her, though, she did not ask. She just wanted to attack him.

'You're not even here, are you? Where are you?' she said.

'Why would I go there, so near to the Sword of Fire, when I know you can destroy me with it?'

'So you're not even in the Black Castle?'

'Appearances can be deceiving.'

'What about all that stuff about heroes?' blurted out Martina. 'Everything you said in Kelytong about sacrificing yourself for everyone else. What happened to all that?'

'You think I don't care about all the people who live in Novrogod? They would destroy each other if it wasn't for me. There would be no more Wizardry and the people would begin wars in the quest for more. They'd die like rats. They would destroy the little they have; they would annihilate everything. I do not destroy; I look after everything. I take care of the Wizardry, which is all we have left. Isn't all this creating something? I am building a present and a future. It's sad to admit, but a flock needs a shepherd, Martina.'

She looked at him, the flaming Sword in her hand, not knowing whether she was still crying or if she was having a nightmare from which she never seemed to awaken.

'You and I are shepherds,' continued Voraz. 'That is our sacrifice for the greater good.'

Martina shook her head, just as she had done when she was little and didn't like something. Once again she felt the hot tears spilling down her cheeks.

'No . . .'

'You have a mission. Here. With me.'

'I want to go back.'

'Go back? Where to?'

'Home.'

'You really think they will look after you there? You're wrong. All anyone cares about is themselves. There are no heroes. There are barely any shepherds, but *you* are one of them. And here you have everything you could wish for. Here you are special, you are unique. You always will be. Here and only here can you be who you truly are.'

'No,' gasped Martina again. She felt saliva pooling in her mouth.

'There is so much evil in the world, oh Sent One,' continued Voraz. 'So much evil. Everything and everyone is full of it. Accept it or go *kaboom*, as Bernarda would say. But you and I can stop all that. We are guardians, Martina. Guardians.'

Martina looked down at her body, covered with the Butterfly's yellow metal, and saw the burning Sword in her hand. Unexpectedly, Nicole and Nadine popped into her head. Hadn't they said something like that, about being her *guardians* when they took her lunch? At that moment she remembered herself. What was she? Who was she? Where did she come from? Where was she going?

She dropped the Sword, which fell to the ground with a metallic clatter, its flame instantly extinguished. A few seconds later Martina felt back in control.

'No,' she said, her voice firm now.

Voraz sighed and said, 'It's all right. I can't force you. Although of course I'll just have to keep Matías. And your dog. They can't be trusted. I wonder what I'll do with them.'

Martina lowered her head, deep in thought. Beneath her on the stone floor lay the Sword. She dried her tears on the back of her hand, closed her eyes and imagined the Sword floating up before her. When she opened her eyes, the silver blade was there in front of her. In the background, Voraz smiled.

'Where is the Oracle?' asked Martina.

'The Oracle?'

'I want to see it.'

Voraz smiled cautiously. 'Really?'

'That's why I'm here, isn't it? Because really, it's partly mine. Where is it? You haven't hidden that like you've hidden yourself, have you? With a charm?'

'The Oracle is the source of all charms. One cannot put a spell on it.'

'Where is it?'

'You ought to be able to see it. As you said, it's partly yours, after all.'

Martina scanned the room around her, her eyes coming to rest on the stone on which Emelia lay. Out of the corner of her eye she could see Voraz and noticed the smirk on his face. She did the same as she had with the Sword: she simply closed her eyes and imagined the stone softly shifting to the side. There was no doubt in her mind that the Oracle and Emelia were two separate entities and she knew she needed to focus only on the Oracle. Martina simply wished for Emelia to remain where she was and for the Oracle to move to the side, lift and float up before her. A soft scraping of stones was heard as, she imagined, the Oracle slid across the ground to one side, moving away from Emelia. When she opened her eyes, there was the Oracle, Emelia no longer resting on top of it. The princess's body was now suspended a metre and a half above the stone floor.

'Touch it,' offered Voraz. 'And may your greatest wish come true.'

Martina cleared her mind before lowering her fingers and the palm of her hand to the stone's surface. Beneath her touch it felt cold as ice, so cold it burned.

'I made this for you,' said Voraz. 'This is why I brought you here.'

Martina removed her hand.

'Hmm, I don't know,' she said.

'You don't know what?' Voraz asked.

In her mind, Martina felt a sudden, unexpected moment of clarity. A crack of light opened up and dispersed the fog that had surrounded her until that instant. What had previously been chaos and confusion now turned into comprehension. The feeling of always being stuck in a dream, staggering on muddy ground that sucked at her feet, shifted. Voraz was a trickster, and this was just another of his tricks. A riddle to solve.

And, after all, she was an expert in solving riddles.

'I don't know. You seem all-powerful, you want to show me that you are so, but . . .'

'What?'

'Appearances are deceiving.'

'You think I'm trying to deceive you?'

'You did. With your name. And your identity.'

'That was just a means to an end.'

'It was just a riddle, not a means to an end. That's OK, in a way: everybody is a riddle, I'm beginning to understand that. They seem difficult at first, but once you crack them, they are really quite simple.'

Voraz pursed his lips in a gesture that was difficult to interpret.

'Martina, I see you're confused. It's natural. This is a lot to take in and I understand that. But bear in mind that everything I did, I had to do. And it was always, always, keeping in mind a higher purpose.'

'Did you? Did you really have a higher purpose?'

'Of course.'

'I don't think so. I think you just wanted to prove to me that you are invincible, but it's just a show.'

'Because I'm not powerful?'

'Because you're not invincible.'

Voraz took an instant to think. His eyes never left her. Then he said, 'I see. What am I then?'

Martina stared at him and said, 'Afraid.'

'Me? Afraid?'

'Yes.'

'Of what?'

Martina rose up in the air.

'Me.'

'You?'

'Yes.'

'Why would I be afraid of you?

Martina lifted the Sword again and it immediately burst into flame, brilliant in the darkness. She looked at Voraz. Or at his image. She felt clearer and clearer.

'Because you were scared I'd find my own way here, take you by surprise and destroy you.'

Martina smiled.

Voraz didn't really react. He was studying her.

Martina continued, 'You never had a higher purpose. The only reason you prepared all this is because you were scared I would be like you – as strong as you, and then I'd take your place. You said it yourself, *There's so much evil in the world. All anyone cares about is themselves.* But I am nothing like you.'

'Martina –'

'How are you going to stop me if you're not even here?' she asked him.

For a second Voraz didn't respond in any way.

'The truth is, I prefer people to get by as best they can . . .' concluded Martina as she lifted the Sword.

'Martina, wait . . .'

'Without the need for *shepherds* or *guardians*.'

'No-o-o-o-o-o!' roared Voraz.

But it was too late. Martina raised the Sword of Fire above her head and, holding it with both hands, she slammed it down on the Oracle with all her might. The impact made her whole body shudder and she lost her grip on the Sword.

However, the Sword of Fire – the blade that burned under water and turned whatever it touched to ash – had left its mark on the stone. A small mark, not very big, but enough. There was a wound on the Oracle and through the cracks that covered it, rivers of fire now flowed, cutting their way in every direction over the surface, devouring everything and turning the stone to ash.

Rays of a thousand colours and ghostly shapes began

shooting out from the dust. Green, orange, blue, white, turquoise, yellow, red, purple – the colours emerged, slowly at first but soon quicker and quicker until the vessel holding the Wizardry shattered. The castle became a volcano. A volcano of Wizardry.

Soon Martina was surrounded by the energy, which jostled her like the waves on the sea. The inside of the Black Castle disappeared. Martina closed her eyes and thought about Emelia, Matías and Socrates. She wished she could see them again, but above all else she wished them to be well. And then she felt a strong desire to return to her normal everyday life; she imagined her bed and longed to go back to school.

In her mind's eye she saw her mum. She remembered how funny she was and how she always came to her in the night if she awoke with a bad dream about a man cloaked in black.

She didn't think she would ever have that dream again.

Martina opened her eyes and saw that she was flying. It was as if she was watching a film in slow motion, as though she was caught in the middle of an explosion, but one that could not hurt her, quite the opposite. She saw the sky. She wondered when and how she had left the castle, what the castle had even been, but she soon stopped asking questions. The clouds cleared and behind them blazed the heavens, crowned by a radiant sun.

The sea sparkled beneath the beautiful skies and the waves lapped calmly. Martina climbed and climbed, like a bird soaring in the warm air. She soared and soared, flying as if there were no end. And although she could see the sea, beneath her was pure Wizardry, thousands of colours merging together. She felt like she had travelled a long way and yet everything was so distant, like an illusion.

Just then it seemed as if a fine layer of water had settled before her eyes, distorting her vision. Novrogod became a series of fuzzy, shape-shifting outlines. The colours melted into one another; the images deformed. The world to which she belonged and yet did not belong lost focus, diluted in a magical liquid.

It was changing. It was all changing. Like a dream, from out of the haze a familiar bookcase began to trace itself before her, followed by a white painted wall . . . Martina recognized her living room back at home in Montevideo.

She could hardly believe it. She stretched out her left hand and for the second time in her life she felt something elastic, something resistant pressing against her skin, but that finally snapped and tore. Air, fresh air, rushed towards her. Martina propelled herself forward as far as she could, feeling that same resistance all around her. She stretched out her right hand, broke through the delicate membrane and felt around for something to hold on to. She found the familiar edges of Grandma Famke's mirror and thrust herself forward. The film stuck to her face before she burst through it.

After spending all that time away, now she inhaled the delicious and unmistakable scent of home. She was finally out of the mirror and standing on the floor. It was night-time. Everything was quiet and calm, especially compared to the intensity of Novrogod just a few minutes – or seconds? – ago. The contrast was overwhelming and it took Martina a couple of breaths to adapt, to settle her heart, and to acknowledge that she was back again, home again.

She stood motionless, her nerves on edge, as if expecting something else to happen, although she couldn't imagine what, and she felt completely unprepared for it. Nothing happened, though. There were no movements, and the only sound Martina could hear, distant and faint, was that of a cricket – so silent was the city, or at least the neighbourhood.

The darkness, only broken by a few gaps in the slats of the blinds, calmed her down. She wasn't going to turn on the lights because she didn't want to wake her mum, but she could still see herself in the mirror. The first time she had entered that house when they were moving in, she had seen herself as a shadow on the floor. Now she watched the girl in the mirror. Was she the same? Had she changed? Perhaps no real change could be distinguished just by looking at her frizzy hair and slim silhouette, but appearances could be deceiving, she knew that for sure.

It was then that she thought about the Butterfly. She touched her forehead. As expected, it wasn't there. She hadn't noticed when it had detached from her, probably when she was soaring in the Novrogodian sky. She had been wrapped up in Wizardry – that was why she hadn't had to return to the River of Dark Waters to come back – and it would've been hard to notice anything else going on. Martina felt no anxiety over that. The Butterfly belonged in Novrogod; that's where it should stay.

Who couldn't stay there any longer was herself. She didn't want her mother to come downstairs, looking for a glass of water, and find her in those strange clothes.

Still, she hesitated a moment before walking over to the staircase and carefully climbing it – taking care to dodge the creaky step – before she finally reached her bedroom.

She lay down on her bed, exhausted. She was in her own home, in her own bed, just as she had wished, back, well, when was it exactly? It couldn't be true, but there she was. Home.

She looked at the clock. Five past midnight. According to her calculations, only minutes had passed since she had left for Novrogod.

Twenty-six
The Sent One

'Martina?'

The voice sounded annoyed. It was her mum, calling to her from her bedroom.

'Yes?' she replied.

'Are you still awake? You've got school tomorrow.'

'I know, I know. I'm going to bed now.'

'Good. If you don't go to sleep now, it'll be even harder than usual to wake you up tomorrow.'

She had to hide all possible evidence of her trip to Novrogod. Her clothes, for example. She concealed everything in the same wardrobe where she had first found the golden cube, stuffing it all into the top corner where her mum would never look.

In one pocket she found some kerpa, and she smiled at the thought of Matías telling her about how dangerous it could be if there wasn't a bathroom nearby. She felt strangely homesick for Novrogod, even though she had only just arrived back. What had happened to Emelia and Matías? And Socrates? She couldn't remember seeing them once the Wizardry had escaped from the Oracle.

These thoughts suddenly put her in a frenzied state. What if her wish for Matías and Emelia to come back to life hadn't come true? What if all the Wizardry that surrounded her couldn't break the spell? Her mouth grew dry and her breathing got faster. She considered calling Matías at home. But of course she couldn't right now, not at this time of night, not without raising suspicions. What excuse would she have? She'd wake his mum as well. She called his mobile phone instead – hoping just to hear his voice – but it was turned off. She sent him a message but got no answer.

She tried to stop thinking about it. She'd find out soon enough at school tomorrow. She put on her pyjamas in the dark and lay down. But even so, her mind wouldn't switch off and the thoughts continued rattling around.

She rolled over, trying to drop off. A few moments later she heard bare feet on the floor. She closed her eyes and sensed her mum come over to her. She brushed Martina's hair out of her face, kissed her forehead and then went back into her own room. Martina opened her eyes and watched her go.

She got out of her bed and took out her diary. For a second, there in her hands, it felt like it was from another world. She grabbed a pen and wrote:

Dear Diary,
I'm back.

She thought a little more. Then added.

And I'm OK.

She looked at the page, at the round and delicate stroke of her handwriting, half expecting to write some more lines, but those words suddenly seemed enough: *I'm OK.*

She closed the diary, left the pen on the side, then lay down again. After a few moments she smiled, clasped her hands behind her head and looked up at the ceiling. Goose bumps prickled over her skin without her really knowing why.

When she went to school the next day she had still received no signs of life from Matías. Martina felt so nervous she had butterflies in her tummy. Maybe he was running late. The one person, however, who was early was his sister, Nicole. Martina felt like running over and asking after Matías, but she didn't dare. Both Nicole and Nadine watched her with spiteful gazes.

She tried to calm down. If Nicole was there looking so normal, nothing bad could have happened to Matías. Or could it? There was no other option but to wait and see. His mobile phone was still turned off. Her classes drifted past without her really understanding a single word. Her mind was elsewhere. Her history teacher, Ms Dutra, gave her a stern look.

'Martina, you're miles away. It's like you're in another world,' she chided.

Martina shrugged in response, thinking to herself, *That's truer than you could even begin to imagine*.

Lunchtime came round as always. Nicole was still behaving as calmly as ever, and yet Martina felt anxious as she came out into the yard to eat her lunch. She peered inside the plastic lunchbox at the meal her mum had put together for her. Today she had some *milanesa* with potato puree and, in a separate bag, a slice of chocolate cake.

'Hey, Ketchup.' Nadine's voice rang out. 'Let's see, eh? What have we got for lunch today?'

Martina sighed. She'd forgotten about them, temporarily at least.

'I don't know. What did you bring, Nadine?' she replied.

'Don't try to argue with me, Ketchup. I just got low marks in Spanish language class. Hand it over.' And without waiting for a response, she grabbed the container with Martina's food in it. She was just about to leave when she spotted that Martina was hiding a small white paper bag.

'What's that?' she asked.

'What?'

'That thing there. What is it?' Nadine said as tried to get a look.

'Nothing. I don't have anything else.'

'Yes, you do. That little white bag. Give it to me,' she demanded. She didn't wait for Martina to comply; she simply snatched it from Martina's fingers. She opened it and looked furiously at Martina. 'You were hiding *this* from me?' she said.

'Me? Hide something from you?'

Nicole chewed her lower lip.

'Oh, sweetie, you really *are* stupid, aren't you? Did you really think we wouldn't notice? You're so obvious.'

Several other kids eating their lunches nearby stopped chatting to watch what was unfolding. Nadine opened the bag.

'Chocolate cake. You're hiding *chocolate cake* from me?' she hissed, as if Martina had committed the greatest crime in the whole history of humanity. 'What is wrong with you?'

Then her face changed. Martina was smiling at her.

'What are you laughing at, fool?' asked Nadine.

'Me, laugh? I'm not laughing.'

Nadine watched her. She swallowed and her face paled. 'You're heading for a beating, loser,' she said.

Martina shrugged. 'Go for it,' she said simply.

'What are you laughing at?!' repeated Nadine.

'Nothing. I'm just waiting for you to finish eating.'

Nadine frowned, worried now.

'What? What do you mean? I don't understand,' insisted Nadine.

'I can see why you got those low marks in Spanish,' said Martina.

Martina kept her eyes fixed on Nadine's and noticed her pale even more. A thought ran through Martina's head: *I am The Sent One. The one sent from Novrogod to planet Earth.* It had a good ring to it.

'Go on,' she encouraged. 'Take a bite.'

Nicole looked at Martina distrustfully.

'You put something in the food . . .' muttered Nicole.

'Me?' exclaimed Martina, putting on an innocent expression. 'I wouldn't do that.'

'You put something in the food!' burst out Nadine.

'Don't you think it's a shame that people only ever think of themselves?' Martina smiled. 'You can't trust anybody these days.'

Nadine stared at her.

'What's got into you today? Stop being so ridiculous.'

'Whatever. I'm just waiting for you to eat.'

'What did you put in the food?'

'Nothing. Just eat it.'

A proper crowd had now started to gather to watch. Martina noted with pleasure that Nicole and Nadine were looking around nervously.

'There can't be anything in it,' said Nadine, trying to sound more confident than she truly felt. 'You were about to eat it.'

'Very true. Although I also knew that you would come and steal it off me.'

Nadine pondered for a few seconds.

'And what if I hadn't taken it off you?' she said. 'You still wouldn't have had any lunch.'

Martina shrugged again.

'Are you feeling all right, Nadine? You look a bit pale.'

'Course. I'm perfectly fine. Did you put something in the food? Yes or no?'

'Me? No. How could you even think that? Not in there, no.'

'You put something in the food I took yesterday, though? What did you put in it?'

'Nothing. Didn't I already say? Nothing at all. If I'd put something in it, you'd be sick by now.'

Nadine smiled confidently.

'Although . . . there are of course those diseases that you only realize you've got once they're really quite advanced,' continued Martina. 'Parasites that begin to eat you from the inside out, rotting your body, even though you look completely fine from the outside. In fact, are you feeling OK? You don't think there might be something inside you, even though you look perfect on the outside?'

Nadine looked at her, unsure how to react, but her face displayed the repulsion she felt. She dropped the food and ran off, Nicole at her side, without so much as a backwards glance. *There we go,* thought Martina, smiling to herself. *Was it really that easy?*

As she picked up what Nadine had left she heard the people around her laughing. Several faces – even those she still hadn't met – nodded to her. As she walked away they carried on laughing, some incredulous. Just as she was about to start eating she heard a familiar voice.

'You defended yourself well.'

Martina spun round. Her heart leaped with joy and a shiver of goose bumps ran over her body. She felt like she might be floating, that if she took a deep breath she might just float away like a balloon.

'Matías!'

His green eyes were watching her from behind the fence between the school yard and the pavement outside.

'You're here! I wasn't sure if you'd made it back. Are you OK?'

'Yes, all good. The return was really weird this time, though. One moment I was standing there in front of Voraz and then suddenly everything started to go blurry. The next thing I knew, I was coming back through my mirror at home.'

'That's exactly what happened to me!'

'Really?'

'Just like that.'

'But *what* happened to you?'

Martina smiled, her nostrils flaring. She tried to hide it, but her face just wanted to explode into a joyful grin.

'Well, you'll have to tell me about it some time,' Matías said.

'What are you doing out there? Why didn't you come to school today?'

'I pretended I was sick. I don't know how you managed to get up and out. I saw your message, so I thought I'd come and see you.'

'But you didn't reply!'

Matías smiled, then said, 'I wanted to see you, not just write.'

Martina swallowed.

'So, everything's all OK in Novrogod?' she asked.

Matías nodded.

'I guess so. I saw Emelia come back to life just before I arrived back. I don't know exactly what happened, but if it wasn't all right, we wouldn't be here. Speaking of all right, I brought you a surprise.'

'A surprise? For me?'

'What? Don't you like surprises?'

Matías turned and let out a loud whistle. Martina looked down the street and saw four long legs chasing down the pavement, a wet tongue lolling out.

'Socrates!'

The dog ran as fast as he could, his ears flapping in the breeze. He rested his paws on the fence to try and get closer to Martina.

'Don't ask me how he got into our world because I have no idea,' said Matías. 'When I left home to come here I found a dog trotting along the street. At first I thought it looked a bit like Socrates, but I told myself, *No, it can't be*. I looked at the dog again, and as soon as he saw me he came tearing over. I thought he was going to eat me but it was actually Socrates. He's driving me crazy, but I had to bring him to see you.' Matías looked at Martina. 'You don't know how he got here, do you?'

Martina remembered wanting to see Socrates one last time as the Wizardry escaped from the Oracle, and she couldn't help smiling as she wondered whether that might have had something to do with it. But she kept her mouth shut.

'I thought that if you can't keep him, well, perhaps I could,' continued Matías. 'Although my mum hasn't seen him yet. When she does, watch out – she won't be happy. But I really don't care.'

Martina giggled and looked at Socrates. He was sticking his nose through the fence and Martina tickled it.

'Hello boy, hello.'

'Well,' Matías said. 'I can't really stay long. I don't want the teachers to see me.'

Martina nodded.

'One last question before I go,' added Matías. 'What was in that cake? Kerpa, by any chance?'

'I don't know what you're talking about,' said Martina, showing him the cake. 'Do you want some?'

Matías scratched his head.

'No, but thanks anyway. I've just had breakfast.'

'Oh well,' said Martina, taking a big bite and chewing it with pleasure. 'Appearances can be deceiving,' she continued, with her mouth full.

Matías laughed and looked at her for a few seconds in silence. Then he said, 'See you, then.'

Martina smiled and nodded again.

'Come on, Socrates. Let's go,' said Matías.

And with that, true to style, Matías simply turned and walked away. With one last glance at Martina, Socrates trotted after him.

THE END